Mills & Boon
Best Seller Romance

A chance to read and collect some of the best-loved novels from Mills & Boon—the world's largest publisher of romantic fiction.

Every month, four titles by favourite Mills & Boon authors will be re-published in the *Best Seller Romance* series.

A list of other titles in the *Best Seller Romance* series can be found at the end of this book.

Anne Hampson

FOLLOW A SHADOW

MILLS & BOON LIMITED
LONDON · TORONTO

First published 1971
Australian copyright 1982
Philippine copyright 1982
This edition 1982

ISBN 0 263 73920 1

Set in Linotype Baskerville 10 on 11pt.
02-0782

Made and printed in Great Britain by
Richard Clay (The Chaucer Press) Ltd.
Bungay, Suffolk

CHAPTER ONE

THE man making his way through the woods halted abruptly as he reached an open glade. His head was cocked, his ears alert, but no sound reached him save the moan of the wind through the trees and the soft lapping of the waves as they broke on to the stony shore of the lake. Overhead the clouds hung low, a snow-laden canopy for the ragged summits of the dark and sombre hills. For a long while he stood motionless, a scowl twisting the ruthless lines of his face, his black eyes moving slowly, searching the trees as if expecting some spectre to appear from behind one of the gaunt misshapen trunks. Then, with a sigh half puzzled, half impatient, he went on his way. Two soft brown eyes followed the tall and arrogant figure, then a slender young body rose from its crouched position and disappeared farther into the woods.

Laura Vernon reached her cottage, pushed open the door and entered. In the shining black-leaded grate a fire burned cheerfully, throwing into relief the picture on the opposite wall, a fifteenth-century oil painting of the Madonna and Child. On the heavy oaken dresser stood an exquisite eighteenth-century 'Queen's Ware' basket-work bowl on a matching stand, and on a shelf in the corner stood a French bracket clock in a Buhl case. The door swung gently to behind her and Laura went over to a small desk and took out a diary. In it she wrote, briefly, 'Saw William today.'

She was about to go into the kitchen to make herself a cup of tea when there was an imperative rapping on the door. She opened it wide and invited her visitor to enter.

'Do sit down, Mr. Crossley. Would you like some

tea? I'm just putting the kettle on.'

'I don't want tea, miss, thank you.' He stood with his back to the fire, hat in hand, a dark and worried frown on his weather-beaten face. 'Have you made up your mind yet?'

A tiny sigh of exasperation left her lips; she continued to stare at the bailiff for a moment and then her eyes travelled to thé window. Through the gathering gloom she could just discern the outline of the house. Mysterious and sinister, it had clung tenaciously to the rocky crags for more than seven hundred years. Fenstone Abbey, once heavily fortified against the lawless Border raiders, it was now almost in a state of disrepair, its towers cracked and seamed, its immense hews forming a barrier against the light, its interior as cold and repellent as those who dwelt within it. 'The Evil Dewars' was the name by which they were dubbed by the tenants on the estate. The Evil Dewars ... descendants of that Red de Warre, kinsman of the Conqueror and so called because his hands were stained with the blood of a hundred victims of his sadism. Through his vast domain he would ride, ordering the torture and death of any serf who, dying from starvation, would dare to poach his rabbits or his deer.

'I've told you so many times, Mr. Crossley. I shall stay in my home——'

'But me, miss,' he interrupted urgently, mopping his brow. 'What about my position? Mr. Bren, he won't believe that I can't get you to go. This is his cottage and he wants it for an estate worker.'

'This cottage belongs to me,' she told him calmly. 'I don't seem able to convince you. Will you ask Mr. Dewar to call on me, please?' Her face was pale, but there was a calmness about her and her dark head was proudly raised. 'I can explain if I see him.' She paused in indecision and then, 'I went out and saw him today——'

'You see him every day—or so the rumour goes,' he interrupted, eyeing her curiously.

This brought a faint flush rising beneath the delicate peach colouring of her face, but her calm demeanour was preserved.

'It was my intention to approach him today, but he looked so——' She broke off, frowning. She could not bring herself to tell Bren Dewar's bailiff that her courage had failed her. 'I feel I shall be able to talk to him with more ease if I do it in my own home.'

'Miss Vernon . . .' He spread his hands entreatingly. 'Mr. Bren won't come here—I daren't even make the suggestion. It would be quite beneath his dignity to come—at the beck and call of one of his tenants, as you might say.'

'I'm not one of his tenants.' Her brown eyes glinted. 'This is my cottage, and I can prove it. As for Mr. Dewar's not being willing to visit me, then I have no more to say.'

'Look,' he persevered desperately, 'you haven't paid your rent for two months. That's grounds enough for getting you out. You'll have to go.'

'I'll pay the rent when I've sold my hens and ducks at Christmas,' she promised. 'But I'm not unduly worried about the rent because I shouldn't be paying any at all.' She paused, struck now by the harassed expression on the bailiff's face. 'What exactly did Mr. Dewar say when you told him I wouldn't leave?'

'He threatened to sack me. Stood there, amazement on his face, and said, so softly, "How old is this girl?" and when I told him he said, in that same soft voice, "Do you mean to tell me that a girl of eighteen has you beaten?" I then had to admit it was so and he said it was time he found himself another bailiff. Her ladyship said I must throw your things into the road—but I couldn't do that, miss, not for anything.'

'Throw my things into the road?' Laura's proud eyes

flashed. 'I wouldn't try, Mr. Crossley, if I were you.'

He became diverted for the moment as his expression changed to one of admiration.

'You've the heart of a lion, miss,' he couldn't help admitting, 'and I've said the same to Mr. Bren. I told him, too, that you were always so quiet and dignified—but I also told him,' he added ruefully, 'that battling with you was like banging one's head against a brick wall, that I'd never come across a more determined person in my life.'

A faint smile touched the fine outline of her mouth.

'What did he say to that?' she asked, watching him curiously.

'Nothing. His lips just went tight and his eyes glinted. You see, no one has defied him in his whole life until now.'

'I don't want to defy him . . .' Laura spoke to herself, her eyes clouding a little. 'I wish we could come to some amicable arrangement.'

'This cottage is wanted for an employee; I've told you. There's no arrangement. You must go.'

A shrug was the only response and he moved to the door.

'I'm sorry to upset you, Mr. Crossley, and I do hope you won't lose your job on account of me. But I absolutely refuse to leave.'

'That's your last word?'

'My last word is that I would like to see Mr. Dewar.'

Scarcely had the bailiff gone than she had another visitor; this was Mr. Dodd, her nearest neighbour. Over eighty years of age, he walked with the aid of a stick.

'Come in,' she called from the kitchen as she recognized the sharp rap of his stick on the door. Taking down a pint mug from a shelf, she placed it on the tray beside her own cup and saucer. 'You must have known I was making tea, Mr. Dodd.' Smiling at him from the kitchen door, she went on to ask about his wife's arthritis. 'Is it still as painful?' she added on an anxious note.

'Always will be.' The old man sat down by the fire, dropped his stick on to the rug and brought a noxious-looking pipe from his pocket. 'Mind if I smoke?'

She shook her head and smiled again. He was already striking the match.

'I've some eggs for her; I'll give them to you—or would you like me to come and see her?'

'She's a-lying down today, so I'll take them. And it's generous you are, young Laura.' A pause, as he regarded her from under ferocious grey brows, his blue eyes deep-set and piercing. A typical Dodd, mused Laura, experiencing no difficulty in seeing his lawless ancestors riding the foray to raid and pillage their unfortunate neighbours' land. But the Vernons had been no better, she thought ... and the Dewars had been the most bloodthirsty of all the Border raiders. 'Saw you coming in a little while ago,' he went on curiously. 'People *know*, young Laura.'

She turned back into the kitchen and lifted the boiling kettle from the oil stove.

'What do they know, Mr. Dodd?' She poured the water into the teapot and laid the kettle on the brown earthenware sink.

'They know as you watches him every day when he takes his walk. I've seen you myself.' He waited as she brought in the tray and placed it on a small table by the wall. 'No good, those Dewars; no better now than when they was engaged in massacre and burning. No wonder most of them ended up on the block.'

Laura sat down on the opposite side of the fireplace, her cup and saucer in her hand.

'Many of your ancestors hanged from the gallows tree,' she reminded him with a laugh. 'And it was a much more honourable death to have your head chopped off. But of course,' she added, her chin lifting with a hint of pride, 'the Dewars were the aristocracy.'

He gave a derisive click of his tongue and took a long drink from his mug.

'Didn't set a very good example, for all that. And what about them now? Still the aristocracy, but as queer birds as ever you would find in the whole of Northumberland.' He took another drink, then leant towards her in a confiding gesture. 'Something funny going on at the Abbey at present. Mrs. Charlton cleans up there—you knows, of course. Well, she comes along and tells my old lady all about the row what went on yesterday morning between Mr. Bren and his aunt. Heard it all, she did, because they was fairly going at each other something terrible. All over the title, it was. Aye, that perishin' title what her ladyship gets all worked up over.' He put his mug to his mouth again and there was silence in the room for a while. Laura gazed pensively into the fire, seeing the dark and arrogant face of Bren Dewar's aunt. It was well known on the estate that she had an obsession about the title's becoming extinct. But strangely, her son, Francis, remained unmarried, it being rumoured that he had periodic fits of insanity. He was supposed to spend these spells in a specially padded room, but no one really knew whether or not these rumours were true. Laura's father had emphatically declared that they were not, but Laura suspected that loyalty to the Dewars might have been the basis for this assertion. However, no one had ever seen Francis as any other than a most charming young man. He was handsome too—far different from his cousin, whose face seemed to reflect all the fiendish cruelty and lawlessness of his barbarian ancestry. 'It seems,' continued the old man presently, 'that her ladyship was saying she'd marry Mr. Francis off to someone, and before very long. "If it's only to the gardener's daughter," she says, and my goodness, was Mr. Bren mad! "That red-faced wench?"

he roars. "You must be out of your mind!" and at that his aunt laughs and says if he doesn't like the idea, then perhaps he can find someone more suitable.'

'And did Bren—Mr. Dewar say he would find someone more suitable?'

'Didn't say anything definite—not just then, at any rate, but swore he'd have no country bumpkin's offspring living in his house.' A broad grin spread over the wrinkled, sallow face. 'He made some pretty disparaging remarks about Mr. Francis's capabilities regarding—er—well, being able to produce an heir.'

'Does the Abbey belong to Mr. Bren?' Laura inquired, flushing slightly at the old man's outspokenness, but quite able to visualize the scene he described. She could actually see the sneer on Bren Dewar's face as he hurled those derisive remarks at his aunt.

'The house and almost the entire Dewar fortune went to Mr. Bren, who ran the estate for his uncle. Lady Margaret and her son were left just enough so as they couldn't oppose the will, but there's some as says their share's gone already, and as Mr. Bren now holds the purse-strings his word's law in everything that goes on up there. The only thing he has no say in is their right to live at the Abbey. His uncle left it as how they was allowed to live there all their lives.'

'Their money's gone, you say? What on?'

'Dunno——' He broke off and laughed. 'May be one or other of them's a secret drinker.'

Laura ignored that as she said musingly,

'It was odd for him to will it to his nephew, don't you think? It's not often a man leaves his money like that.'

'Rumour has it that he didn't believe Mr. Francis to be his son. Said once that there never was insanity in the Dewar family—nor had there been any in his wife's family. So he wondered where Francis had got it from.' He grinned again. 'Women certainly have the advantage there. I expect there have even been kings who, if the truth were known, had no right to the crowns they wore.'

'It's a shame, really,' said Laura, ignoring those last remarks, 'that the money was all left away from Francis. The house is falling into ruin, for Bren won't spend a penny on it—at least, that's what people say, and it must be true, otherwise he'd have had the place repaired and put into some sort of order.'

'He hates it; that's what he told her ladyship last night.'

'Then why doesn't he leave, I wonder?' But a frown crossed her brow at the idea of such a possibility.

'Don't see how he can, seeing that the estate belongs to him. He runs it—with the help of Mr. Crossley, that is. If he left he'd have to sell the lot, and I can't see him doing that. Been in the family too long.' He drained his mug with much more noise than was necessary and placed it on the hearth. 'Besides,' he added, 'that place suits Mr. Bren's personality. Evil it is, like him.' Leaning forward, he picked up his stick. 'Wonder if we'll be having a wedding here soon?'

Automatically she shook her head.

'I somehow feel Francis will never marry.'

'Don't you be too sure. True, none of the nobs will let their daughters marry into such a family, but you can take my word for it, her ladyship's in real earnest this time. She'll have that buxom wench, if it's only to spite Mr. Bren.'

'But you've just said he objects to her.'

'True, he does; so perhaps he'll have a look round for someone with a—what do you say?—a little more culture, a lass who's a little more refined, so to speak.' He wagged a finger at her. 'You mark my words, he'll find someone for Mr. Francis.' The old man rose from the chair with difficulty and Laura moved, offering a helping hand. 'Thanks, you're a nice little lass.' His glance strayed to the bookshelves lining one wall. 'Do you read those, or are they there because your father left them?'

'They're there because Daddy left them, but I read them.' She sighed and for the first time the hint of a shadow crossed her face. 'There isn't anything else to do, now that I'm quite alone.'

'How long is it now, young Laura?'

'Six months. I do miss him ... we were so very close.'

'Should get yourself a nice young man—there are several on the estate who'd be glad to go a-courting with a lovely lass like you.' He stood by the door looking at her for a moment and then, 'But you're a bit uppish, you know, young Laura. Sort of haughty.'

'Haughty—oh no, Mr. Dodd, I'm not in the least haughty.'

'Proud, then ... as if you was the aristocracy yourself, if you know what I mean.'

Faintly she smiled and her eyes strayed to the other door, the one leading to the tiny parlour. And then she caught sight of herself in the mirror; she turned her head this way and that, proudly noting the fine lines of her face, the high sweep of her forehead, the long curve of her neck.

'I don't want to go a-courting with a boy from the estate,' she declared emphatically. 'I think I shall die an old maid, Mr. Dodd.'

'Not you, young Laura,' came the swift response. 'No—never!'

Laura opened up the shed and drove the ducks through the snow and on the pond. This way their keep cost nothing, for they found their natural food. In a week, though, she must begin supplementing their diet in order to fatten them. She went back and fed the hens and after collecting the eggs she trudged through the snow to the house. Pity the snow had come so early;

it did lengthen the winter so. The door was open and a frown touched her brow. She had closed it . . .

She stood on the threshold, staring at the man standing by the desk. She had left her 'diary' on top and he had it in his hands. Laura smiled faintly as she imagined his reading 'Saw William today' and the next line, 'Saw William today' and the next line, and the next . . .

She stamped the snow off her shoes, entered the living-room, and closed the door quietly behind her. The man turned, his arrogant gaze sweeping over her before coming to rest on her face. She wondered if she imagined it, but he seemed to give a little start of amazement.

'Mr. Dewar . . .' She inclined her head slightly in a gesture of respect, but showed no evidence of surprise. 'I'm sorry I wasn't here when you arrived. Have you been waiting long?'

Bren Dewar stiffened haughtily.

'You were expecting me?'

'Naturally. A meeting between us was essential.' She wasn't in the least dashed by the sudden raising of his eyebrows. 'I asked Mr. Crossley to tell you I would like to see you. He seemed afraid to do so, but I knew that in the end he'd have no alternative.'

'Miss Vernon——' His narrowed gaze was almost threatening. 'It is not usual for my tenants to summon me into their presence,' he informed her icily, and at that her colour did begin to heighten.

'I hope I haven't annoyed you too much, Mr. Dewar, but I wished to speak to you about the cottage and I didn't think you'd like me to come up to your house.' She spoke in a low and softly modulated tone, and with an accent far removed from that of the rest of his tenants. 'Won't you sit down?' She drew out a chair, but he was not looking either at her or the chair. His eyes were fixed on the clock in the corner. Obviously he hadn't been in the room many moments before she arrived, as he hadn't looked around. He did so now and his gaze rested for a moment on the painting before moving to the Wedgwood basket on the dresser. 'Please sit down.'

He remained standing, his gaze returning to Laura; he seemed to be curious both about her and the treasures he saw in this tiny stone cottage.

'You wished to speak to me, you said? Please proceed.'

'It's just that I don't intend leaving my home——'

'You'll leave this house because I say so. As you know, my bailiff looks after these things for me. What do you mean by defying him?'

'I don't want to leave my home,' she said, staring at him gravely. 'Would you like to leave yours?' Perhaps he would, she thought, seeing that it was so grim, and with an aspect so sinister and dark.

'You're impertinent! This cottage belongs to me. I want possession of it by the end of the year.'

Laura flinched under his tone; despite her intention of keeping calm her hands began to twitch convulsively and she found herself apologizing for the arrears of rent.

'I'll pay when I sell my fowls at Christmas——'

'I'm not concerned about the rent. I've a man waiting to come into this cottage—he's been waiting quite a while,' he reminded her grimly. 'But I waste time, my bailiff has told you all this.'

'Indeed he has,' she responded feelingly. 'Several times—and I'm sorry to cause all this trouble, but I can't leave my home.' She touched the back of the chair as if hoping he would sit down. He still remained standing and she went on, 'I was born here, and generations of my people before me—for two hundred years we've lived in this cottage and I feel I've a right to stay, even though it was my father who was the tenant. I feel the cottage belongs to me.'

His eyes held a curious expression as he glanced at the painting on the wall opposite.

'And I *know* that it belongs to me. You'll be out by the end of next month.'

Again she flinched and a hint of pain actually touched the soft brown eyes, but only fleetingly. She saw his expression change as her own became defiant, the pain in her eyes changing to a sparkle of militance.

'My people have lived in this cottage for two hundred years,' she repeated. 'I'm entitled to stay here just as long as I like—and I might as well tell you it will be for the rest of my life.'

'You——!' His face darkened and his tone was intended to make her tremble in her shoes. 'I'm not in the least interested in your forebears, Miss Vernon! My last word has been said on the matter!' He strode to the door.

'Mr. Dewar...'

He turned.

'No hard-luck stories, please. You haven't lived here for eighteen years and not heard of my reputation. If it's pity you want, then you can save your breath.'

'Pity!' she flashed, drawing herself up in a manner almost as arrogant as his own. 'I have no need of your pity!' Her gaze was unflinching as she went on to tell him she hadn't the slightest intention of leaving the cottage, and she added, 'You daren't send anyone here to remove my possessions!'

Slowly he came back into the room to stand very close, towering above her, his black eyes hard as flint.

'Do you imagine,' he said softly, 'that I shall allow a child like you to defy me?'

Laura stepped back against the table, one hand clutching the back of a chair as though for support, but the militant sparkle still shone in her eyes.

'I don't want to defy you,' she told him quietly. 'I'd

hoped it wouldn't be necessary for me to do so. That was why I wanted to see you and talk this over—I thought you'd be kinder—more understanding—than Mr. Crossley.'

His lips curled sardonically.

'I just asked if you'd heard of my reputation. Do I appear to be kind and understanding?'

She examined the features she knew so well.

'No, but I hoped ... I somehow *felt* you would understand.'

'Then I'm at a complete loss to know why. My—heartlessness is common knowledge for miles around.'

'I don't believe all I hear.' A strange little smile hovered on her lips. 'I like to judge for myself.'

'Then you have the opportunity of judging me now. I want possession of this cottage and I mean to have it.'

She stood motionless by the table, her face had paled and her fingers continued to move convulsively.

'Is there nothing I can do to make you change your mind? If I tell you——?'

'That you have no money, no relatives.' A laugh grated on her ears. 'My good girl, I've just warned you not to try any of those hard-luck stories on me. You've already tried to soften my bailiff with them.'

'I've never tried to soften Mr. Crossley with a hard-luck story! How dare he tell you such a thing!' Her fists clenched and for a moment he looked as if he expected to see one of them come crashing down upon the table. 'How *dare* he!'

Bren seemed slightly taken aback; things weren't going quite as he expected, she thought, not without satisfaction.

'You told him you'd no relatives.'

'Because he asked me. You don't expect me to lie, do you? As for having no money—I have a fortune, a *fortune*, understand that!'

'Indeed?' Unveiled amusement lit his eyes. 'Then why don't you pay your rent?'

A long, thoughtful silence followed and then, quietly,

'I had hoped it wouldn't be necessary for me to disclose certain facts, but you're compelling me to do so.' Walking over to the other door, she opened it. There was nothing in the tiny parlour except an enormous painting almost covering one wall. 'Will you step over here?'

Bren shot her a curious glance, then complied with her request.

'What——?'

'Do you recognize him?' A slender hand gestured towards the painting. 'You have portraits of your ancestors up at the Abbey.'

Bren stood rooted to the floor, and it was a long while before he said, uncomprehendingly,

'This is William Dewar, fourth baron, and yet...' He turned to her. 'What is it doing here? Where did it come from?'

'It was painted by an unknown artist,' she informed him, almost reverently. 'A peasant girl by the name of Laura Vernon, a girl with whom William was in love. You will recollect that my name is also Vernon?' and at that his black eyes widened with perception.

'Please come to the point,' he encouraged, amused.

'I shall prove that this cottage is mine. Will you sit down while I tell you about it? Perhaps you would like some tea?'

'I would not,' he declined crisply. 'And after all, I don't think I need hear more. You're descended from one of William Dewar's illegitimate children—one of them, mark you—and you think that gives you the right to this house.' He looked down at her flushed face with considerable amusement. 'If every descendant of William Dewar claimed part of this estate there'd be nothing left.'

'I've no wish to claim this cottage as my own,' she reminded him gently. 'I merely want to remain . . . as a tenant.'

'Well, you're not going to; this makes no difference whatever. Did you really believe it would?'

'Will you please let me finish?'

'There's no need; I understand perfectly. It's an interesting theory you have, Miss Vernon, but one that isn't going to serve.'

'You haven't heard the whole story,' she persevered desperately. 'If you will listen you'll realize that this cottage really belongs to me.'

'I've neither the time nor the inclination to listen to the amorous stories of my——' He broke off and his laugh echoed through the room. 'Our ancestor, Miss Vernon. Good afternoon.'

'I'll buy the cottage—I'll give you anything you ask! Ten thousand pounds, twenty thousand . . .'

Bren turned. 'Miss Vernon,' he said in a wondering tone, 'I do believe you're trying to pull my leg!'

'I'm not, indeed I'm not. Wait one moment——' She looked at him imploringly. 'Don't go—please. I won't be a minute.'

She sped upstairs; there was the sound of an iron bedstead being moved and the rattle of floorboards being taken up; a few moments later Laura returned carrying a wooden box which she placed on the table. The lid was removed. Inside were several jewel cases, all of which she brought out before opening any of them.

'This is a necklace—diamonds.' She thrust the case into his hands. 'Take it. How much is it worth? Is it enough? This bracelet—rubies, aren't they? Will those two buy the cottage?'

He was fingering the jewels, his face a dark mask of suspicion.

'What else have you there? Show me,' he demanded sternly, and Laura brought another necklace from its bed of velvet. It was a diamond one, like the first, but with finer, larger stones.

'I'll give you all those. Surely they'll buy the cottage?'

He stared at the necklace, for the moment bereft of speech.

'Good God!' he exclaimed at last. 'All this is part of the Dewar collection, stolen over a hundred years ago! Offer them to me for the cottage, would you?' he added grimly. 'Let me have a look at the others.'

'Stolen! How dare you accuse me of having stolen property in my possession? These were given to my great-grandmother by William; he loved her. I tried to tell you the whole story, but you wouldn't listen. They were to be married—— Oh yes, they were! What are you doing? You can't take them from me, they're mine—*mine,* I tell you!' She snatched at the case he was putting in his pocket; failing to recover it, she made a grab at one of the cases lying on the table. His fingers closed like a vice on her wrist, the pressure increasing mercilessly until she cried out and dropped the case back on to the table. Her lips quivered and a look of anguish filled her eyes. 'You wouldn't take them from me,' she cried, rubbing her wrist soothingly and then clasping her hands together in a gesture of entreaty. 'Not you—you wouldn't, no, not you . . .'

'Certainly I would.' His eyes were as cruel as the grip that had so savagely bruised her. 'I take what's my own.'

Laura was stunned, though after a moment she thought of those other Dewars, plunderers of their neighbours' property; those lawless vagabonds, those 'wild and misdemeanoured people'. So wicked they were that it was said their souls couldn't rest, that in October when the hunter's moon was full, their ghosts could be seen riding, headless, over the lands they had pillaged and burned.

In spite of this, she could not see this man taking her property, stealing from her what was rightfully her own.

'If someone else stole them from me it wouldn't matter . . .' Her voice became a pleading whisper. 'But not you. Please, *please* give them back to me.' And when he shook his head, 'It isn't the value, not even the sentimental value, but—but something I can't explain.' Without thinking she put out a hand and touched the fingers that held the bracelet. 'When I fetched them for you to see I had no fear that you would steal them from me. I trusted you. I'd gladly give them to you, but please don't steal them.'

'You would . . . give them to me?' he echoed incredulously. 'Do you know what they're worth?'

'I said I had a fortune,' she reminded him with a forced little smile. 'I know they're valuable, but I must admit I don't know their actual worth. You see, no one, other than my own family, has ever seen them since they were given to Laura.'

'You persist in this ridiculous story?'

'I can prove they were gifts. I have letters and a diary.'

'And yet you'd give them to me?' His tone was sceptical as, unconsciously, his eyes strayed to the 'diary' on top of the desk.

'I don't really want to part with them,' she said earnestly. 'But I'd much rather give them to you than have you steal them from me.'

'If you have this proof, I can't steal them from you. You could claim them back.'

'You mean—charge you with theft? I could never do that, not to you.'

'Why me?' he asked strangely. 'You mean that if someone else stole them you'd make a charge?'

'Certainly, if I knew who it was.'

'Then why not me?' His tone held a curious ring and he shook his head uncomprehendingly. 'I fail to see why it should make any difference.'

'It's something I can't explain.' Laura flushed and turned away. 'Please don't ask me.'

'But I want to know,' he persisted. 'What makes me so different from anyone else?'

After a long moment of hesitation she said evasively, 'It's because we're related—distantly, it's true, but related for all that.'

Bren sat down, regarding her inscrutably for some moments in silence.

'A most unsatisfactory answer,' he said at length, 'because you don't know me at all. We're complete strangers. However, your explanation will suffice for the time being. Now please let me have your story.'

The jewel cases were all together at his elbow, as if ready to be picked up and taken away. One necklace lay on the table, out of its case.

'My jewels?' she began, when he interrupted her.

'If they're yours you shall keep them, but I've no intention of taking your word alone; I must see these letters and the diary, for I find it impossible to believe William Dewar would give these things to one of his—— Well, you'd better begin your story.'

As she drew the wooden box towards her he saw at once that it had a false bottom. Removing it, she produced two bundles of faded letters and a leather-bound diary; these she put trustingly into his hands.

She saw him frown at her action. The jewellery, the letters and the diary . . . he had only to keep them all. Perhaps he was thinking she was very foolish, too childishly trusting. Ah, but he didn't know . . .

'You'll be able to piece the story together from those, but they'll take some time to read so perhaps you'd like to take them home.' She hesitated. 'You'll return them to me?'

'I shall return them intact,' he promised. 'And now, your story, please.'

'It's been handed down by word of mouth,' she began. 'If I tell it to you that way you'll better be able to understand the diary, for there are a few incidents which Laura Vernon left out. I think you'll already know that as a youth William Dewar was a weakling; he also lacked strength of character. His younger brother was the strong man of the family.' She smiled faintly, directing her glance to the door of the parlour, and for a moment she strayed from the point. 'That portrait is a combination of the two,' she went on dreamily. 'I think Laura Vernon painted William as she would have liked him to be and not as he really was. Perhaps you noticed the eyes and the chin?'

He nodded, clearly absorbed in her story.

'I did. I thought it was meant to be a portrait of William, but it's not like any we have at the Abbey. I concluded that it was just a bad painting.'

'I think it was done intentionally. Laura combined the good looks of one brother with the firmness of the other...' Another pause and a dreamy smile. 'The likeness to yourself is rather striking, don't you think?'

'I'm extremely flattered, Miss Vernon,' he answered dryly. 'Er—I am not considered good-looking—just the reverse, in fact.'

She examined his face, so dark and arrogant; he didn't care a damn whether he were considered good-looking or not!

'I think you are,' she returned, without embarrassment. 'People's ideas about such things differ.' That dry expression returned to his eyes and Laura resumed her story. 'William's love for Laura changed his way of life completely. Until then he had, as you hinted, been something of a—a rake. But from the time he met her she was the only one. However, much as he loved her he hadn't the courage to present her to his people. I expect he knew they would never accept her. Meanwhile his father and mother were arranging for his marriage to a nobleman's daughter, and he became engaged to her.' She smiled at Bren, her eyes bright, and clear with the innocence of youth. 'You see, he was improved in health, but nothing could strengthen his character; he was still a weakling when it came to standing up to his family—which was not at all characteristic of the—the——' She broke off and he added softly,

'The bloodthirsty Dewars? The clan who feared no man either side of the Border?' He was obviously amused, and she laughed. His eyes took on an odd expression as he watched her.

'His family arranged everything,' she went on. 'The wedding date was fixed and you'll see from the diary what suggestions he made to Laura.' A flush crept to her cheeks at the mention of this and for a moment she lowered her head, hiding her confusion. 'Laura would have none of it; if he married this other woman he must remain faithful to her. Well, he evidently found it impossible to give Laura up and he agreed to marry her secretly at the home of a friend. On the way to the wedding——' She stopped, and a sadness crept into her voice. 'You know the rest. The coach overturned and he was killed.'

Bren was silent for a space and then he said quietly, 'I'm aware that William was killed, but I've no reason to believe he was on his way to his wedding.'

'It's all in the diary. Laura was flung clear; they were only about half a mile from their destination and she went for help. William died at the home of his friend —died in Laura's arms. The last thing he did was to return her letters—he carried them about with him— and——' She broke off, swallowing convulsively. 'His wedding present to her was this necklace. The other jewellery he gave to her at various times, as you will see from the diary. His last wish was for her to have the cottage. "Tell your father to go up to the Abbey and see my parents about it," he said, but this friend advised her to go home and say nothing to anyone. He was probably thinking William's people would mete out some punishment to Laura, as she was having a baby. She took his advice, for she suspected they would never give her the cottage.' Absently she fingered the necklace, her thoughts dwelling on the tragedy that had brought such sorrow to that first Laura Vernon, the lovely young peasant girl who had been so near to becoming the mistress of Fenstone Abbey. 'This was the story I meant to tell you—but only if I failed to persuade you by any other means to let me stay here. I think you'll now agree that the cottage really belongs to me.'

Bren Dewar was staring at the letters and the diary in his hand; he appeared to have missed her last remark. 'I didn't intend to mention the jewels or the letters because I thought you'd believe my story and let me stay. But when you wouldn't even listen, I became desperate, and that's why I offered to buy the cottage.'

Still he remained lost in thought, but after a while his lips moved and he muttered to himself,

'If William had lived another hour there'd have been none of this anxiety over the title...' He looked up sharply as if struck by some idea and his keen gaze became fixed on Laura in a prolonged and searching scrutiny. 'The title...' When at last he stood up all his cool arrogance had returned.

'An interesting story, very interesting. I'll take these home and read them.'

'You'll let me stay here?'

He looked again at the wealth on the table.

'Is that all you want? Have you no ambition? These

would realize a considerable sum of money; you could invest it and live comfortably for the rest of your life.' His glance fell on the notebook on top of the desk. 'Perhaps you're thinking of getting married?'

She looked up quickly, the soft colour tinting her cheeks.

'I shall never marry,' she replied firmly, and one of Bren Dewar's rare laughs echoed through the tiny room.

'You're much too young, and much too beautiful to be able to say a thing like that.'

'Thank you.' Her prim tones added to his amusement. 'But I know for sure I'll never marry.'

'You've a boy-friend, though?' he remarked, his glance again flickering to the diary.

'Boy-friend?' She stared at him with a blank expression, then realized what he was thinking and a faint smile touched her lips. 'No, I have no boy-friend.'

His manner became rigid.

'I'll bid you good afternoon, Miss Vernon,' but then he added a trifle anxiously, 'I should put those away at once.'

'You haven't promised to let me stay.' She opened the door for him to pass through. 'I'll pay the rent—truly, when I sell my fowls at Christmas.'

A small moment of silence; his eyes wandered to the table again.

'What a strange girl you are. Why don't you sell one of those useless trinkets and put yourself in the square? What's the sense of all this struggling when, as you remarked yourself, you have a fortune?' He broke off frowning. 'How is it that none of these has been sold before now?'

'Laura Vernon left them to the first female child,' came the simple explanation. 'To me they are of great sentimental value and I shall never sell any of them unless I'm desperate.' She smiled up at him. 'If you won't rent me the cottage I shall have to sell some of them in order to buy it—that is, if you'll sell it to me.'

'I never sell the cottages on my estate,' Bren informed her quietly, 'but you can stay for the time being. I'll send these back in the morning.' The next moment he was striding down the little path towards the gate. She watched him until he was out of sight and then, going back to the cottage and taking the notebook from the desk she sat down at the table and wrote, 'Talked to William this afternoon.'

CHAPTER TWO

LAURA was polishing the brass door-knocker when Bren Dewar called the following day, and she turned, greeting him with a smile.

'Will you come in?' she invited, pushing open the door wider. He entered the room and threw a parcel on to the table.

'You've read the diary and the letters? You're convinced the jewels are mine?'

'I was convinced before I read the letters,' he admitted. 'Yes, the jewellery belongs to you.'

From somewhere at the back there came the delicious smell of freshly baked cakes. Laura looked at Bren and said, on a note of faint entreaty,

'Will you have a cup of tea?'

He surveyed her coolly before nodding his acceptance; her eyes lit up as she sped away to the kitchen.

'It won't take a minute,' she called over her shoulder. 'The kettle's already boiling.' She had more than the water prepared and within a very short while she was taking the tray into the room. It was daintily set with fine china cups and saucers, and a plate of cakes.

'Do you have sugar?' she inquired, in her low and softly modulated voice.

'One, please.' His eyes seemed to be riveted on the lovely china; he was about to make some comment on it, but changed his mind.

'Were you going to remark on the cups?' she queried, passing him the cakes with all the assurance of the experienced hostess.

He smiled faintly. 'I was about to say they are very old and beautiful—and we have some exactly the same up at the Abbey.' His dark eyes actually twinkled for a second. 'Our set is incomplete.'

'William gave these to Laura's mother for her silver wedding present,' she informed him demurely.

'William was certainly generous,' was Bren Dewar's dry comment. 'Have you anything else?'

'Only some small ornaments William gave Laura for her bedroom. We had them in the sitting-room until Father's illness,' she added, her face clouding as she fell silent for a space. 'But we had to sell the furniture to pay for his needs. I have them in my room now. Would you care to see them?'

'Yes—yes, I would.'

She fetched the china figures for him, placing them carefully on the table. Bren picked one up.

'Chelsea china ... My dear girl, why do you live with all this poverty?' His gesture embraced the whole room. 'What on earth made you sell your furniture when you had all these?'

'Laura's possessions are of great sentimental value to me,' she told him solemnly. And then, shaking off the momentary sadness that had entered into her, 'Will you have a cake?'

'Thank you.' Bren Dewar was looking at her closely, a very odd expression in his eyes. He examined her hands, so slender and white, so beautifully kept despite her fowls and all the work they entailed. He watched her face in profile, her lovely face with its fine contours and delicate lines. She became aware of his interest and smiled; her dark eyes smiled too and he caught his breath. He returned the ornament to the table and accepted the cake offered to him. Laura put the plate back on the tray and waited expectantly, her eyes never leaving his face as he took a bite out of the cake. Her expectancy dissolved when it became apparent he was to make no comment on her baking.

'Sentimental value or not,' Bren mused, staring at the figures as if his thoughts had been on them all the time, 'I still think you should have sold some of these things and given yourself a little comfort.'

She shook her head, and her shining dark hair fell over one shoulder, draping itself across the tender curve of her breast, as if to shield it from the gaze of this man whose eyes were now examining every detail of her slender figure.

'As I've said, all Laura's things are of great sentimental value to me——' She broke off and then continued with a sudden twinkle, 'I'm romantic and sentimental; I can't help it, because of my name.'

'Your name——?' He paused. 'Is your name Laura?'

'But of course,' she replied, as though it could not possibly be anything else.

'What a strange family you must have been,' he murmured reflectively. 'Did none of the others ever think of selling any of these treasures?'

'They couldn't. You remember, I told you they had to come down to the first female child.'

'The jewellery, yes, but these . . .?'

'We seem to have made a saint of Laura, and this cottage has always been regarded as a sort of shrine.' She now spoke matter-of-factly, helping herself to a cake and regarding it for an instant before putting it to her mouth. 'That's one reason why the cottage is so important to me.' She smiled again, holding his gaze as if she would draw a smile from his lips too. She failed, for his mouth remained firm and set, matching to perfection the harsh and merciless lines of his face.

'Tell me about this family of yours?' he pressed, ignoring her last remark. 'You've no relatives; does that mean you were an only child?'

'I had a brother. He died before I was born.'

'Your father, did he have no brothers or sisters?'

'No. Laura had one son, as also did my grandfather. That's why I've no relatives.'

'I see . . .' He paused an instant, thoughtfully. 'And

that's why you've come into all this wealth. But it's no good to you under the floorboards up there. You must get some of it sold and buy yourself another place.'

'Another place?' Laura went pale. 'Aren't you going to let me stay here, after all?'

'I didn't promise to let you stay here indefinitely,' he reminded her. 'Nothing's changed; I still require this cottage for one of my men.'

'But I couldn't sell anything to buy another place!'

'You were willing to sell some of your jewellery to buy this one—or, at least, you offered to give it to me in exchange, which is the same thing.'

'No——' Laura shook her head emphatically. 'No, it isn't the same at all. This was Laura's cottage—but I couldn't sell anything of hers to buy a strange place—— No, I could never do that!'

He took up his cup and held it to his lips, his eyes on Laura. She had the peculiar conviction that he had known, even before suggesting it, that she would never sell Laura's possessions to buy anything except this particular cottage. Why then had he made the suggestion?

'I'll give you everything—everything...'

'Do you think I would take them from you?'

She lowered her head under the rebuke.

'No—no, I don't.'

'As I said, you can remain here until you find what you want, and then, I'm sorry, but you must go.'

She glanced swiftly at him; again there was something in his manner that convinced her he was deliberately wasting words. He knew without any doubt at all that she would hold on to her treasures, even should he go to the lengths of having her ejected from the cottage. In other words, he knew she would never look for somewhere else to live.

'You would really make me go, after what I've told you?' Her voice held bitter disillusionment and a frown of perplexity crossed his brow. 'You'd turn me out when you know this place really belongs to me?'

Bren replaced his cup and saucer on the tray and moved impatiently.

'The cottage belongs to me.'

'William's last wish was for Laura to have it,' she interrupted hotly. 'It belongs to me, no matter what you say!'

'Be very careful,' warned Bren softly, 'or I might change my mind about allowing you to stay until you've found what you want. I'm not a patient man—and I don't tolerate defiance.'

Her lips trembled; she looked at him through misty eyes.

'Is that your final word?'

'That's my final word,' he returned inexorably.

'Then there's nothing I can do.' Mechanically she picked up the plate and offered him the cakes again. When he shook his head she put it back on the tray. 'You've had only one and I made them specially...' She tailed off and Bren said, an odd inflection in his tone,

'Did you expect me to come this morning?'

'Yes.'

'But I said I'd send your papers back. I didn't say I'd return them myself.'

'No ... but I didn't think you'd trust anyone else with them.'

'I could have trusted my chauffeur with them, but I wanted to see you.'

She lifted her head. 'See me?'

'It isn't at all safe for you to have that jewellery in the house. You must take it to a bank.'

'I haven't a bank. It's been here all these years,' she said listlessly. 'No one would break into a tiny place like this. It's quite safe——'

'My dear girl,' he cut in impatiently, 'do have a little

common sense. No one keeps valuables like that in the house.' A small pause and then, 'Would you like me to take care of them for you—until you decide which items you're deciding to sell?'

'I'm not selling any,' came the firm and stubborn rejoinder, and she added, 'You know I won't part with them.'

He actually gave a slight start, but instantly recovered himself.

'I'm sure I'm not in the least interested in your intentions—but I am interested in obtaining this cottage for my man. You'll oblige me by beginning to look for somewhere else at once.' And with that he rose from the chair, bade her a curt good morning, and left her without another word.

Laura looked mistily round the room, and then at Bren, so tall and dark, his arms full of boxes, carefully and neatly packed.

'I'll put these in the car,' he said. 'Bring out that small suitcase, if you can manage it.'

Perhaps if he had sounded a little more human, had displayed a hint of sympathy and understanding, Laura might have been able to leave without any visible sign of emotion, but at the curtness of his tone she put a handkerchief to her eyes and wept brokenly into it.

This was Bren's first experience of feminine tears, and to all outward appearances he was totally unmoved by them. However, when he returned from putting the boxes in the car she had made some effort at regaining her composure.

'What are these new people like?' she asked, a catch in her voice. 'Are they nice? Will they love this place, d-do you th-think?'

'I've never met the man's wife, or his children, but

the man is one of the most capable workers on the estate.'

'Capable?' She shook her head and a frown of anxiety creased her brow. 'I meant, is he a nice person? Will he love my cottage?'

'I didn't think to ask him.' Reaching for the large suitcase by the wall, Bren drew it into the centre of the room, placing it alongside a battered trunk already lying there. 'Is this the lot?'

'My other box—in the sitting-room.' Tears threatened again as she dwelt on Bren's sarcastic reply to her question. The new people would not love the cottage. she felt sure. They'd merely live in it and probably modernize it until its mellowness, and the influence of Laura Vernon's sweetness would gradually fade and eventually be lost for ever.

She followed Bren as he went into the sitting-room to fetch the box. Over the mantelpiece was a large square of faded, old-fashioned wallpaper. Laura stared at it and the tears rolled down her cheeks again.

'The painting had never been moved since the day it was put up,' she whispered huskily. 'We always papered round it.'

Bren was busy with the lid of the box.

'Mmm ...?' he murmured absently, without looking up.

'The portrait—it hasn't been moved until now.' She spoke in a slightly raised voice, desperately wanting him to take notice of her. 'We always papered round it...' He wasn't listening—or was not interested—for he still remained intent upon his task, and with a final unhappy glance around the tiny room Laura walked out of it for the last time ... or so she believed.

She sat in the car while Bren locked up, and when he dropped the key into his pocket she had to bite her lip hard to prevent the tears falling again.

'I never thought I'd leave,' she said convulsively. 'I

thought I'd live there all my life.' She twisted round as the car reached a bend in the road. There had been a change in the weather, but although the snow had vanished there was a chill in the air and the faintest hint of mist. 'It looks so lonely without the curtains—— And the garden—it looks funny without the hens scratching. Do you think the new people will have hens?'

'Very likely. There's no need for you to strain your neck like that. You're not moving miles away; you can come back and look at it just whenever you like.'

'I don't think I want to see it when the new people have it. They might have lace curtains; most people do, so that you can't see in—and I don't like lace curtains.' She hesitated. 'Do you have lace curtains up at the Abbey? I like flowers, lots of big red ones with green leaves. Perhaps you have flowered curtains,' she added hopefully, although she could not really imagine her hope being fulfilled.

'I'm afraid not, but we don't have lace ones either, so that might be a slight consolation to you.'

'I suppose you have beautiful red velvet ones?'

'I believe they are mostly velvet, but not red. I'm sorry.'

Laura glanced uncertainly at him and lapsed into silence. She had a vague suspicion that he was laughing at her, but after considering this she decided she was mistaken. She very much doubted that he possessed a sense of humour, but even if he did he surely would not laugh at her at a time like this.

Not many minutes passed before the car swung into the drive, swept past the two men brushing dead leaves into a great pile on the grass verge, and came to a stop at the front door of the Abbey.

'You'll call her ladyship Aunt Margaret,' Bren had earlier told her.

'I'm sure I'll have difficulty,' Laura had begun to

protest, but had been curtly interrupted.

'Perhaps; but you'll get used to it.'

Laura had been about to continue her protest when she suddenly remembered that Margaret was Bren's aunt, too, and that made her feel a little happier.

Margaret was now standing in the doorway, cool and dignified and lacking her customary arrogance.

'Come in, my dear,' she invited smilingly. 'You look cold, and not very happy. Was it so dreadful, leaving the cottage?'

Managing a smile, Laura did not speak for a space, as she examined this tall and stately person to whom she was to refer from now as Aunt Margaret.

'Yes, it was...' She stared around her, and shivered. The hall was dark and gloomy, the walls hung with sombre paintings. Through an open door Laura glimpsed a shadowy room with heavy curtains and obscure furnishings. Several corridors led off the hall, dark mysterious corridors which sent a tingle of fear down her spine, and turning, she took an involuntary step towards the door. Bren stood there, tall and gaunt, one of her suitcases in his hand. Dusk was rapidly falling; behind Bren an outside light had been switched on, catching his face in the shadows and giving it a sinister aspect. 'I w-want to g-go b-back...' She pulled herself together, but took another step towards him as if drawn by some irresistible force. 'Have you got everything?' she inquired prosaically.

'The rest of your things will be brought in directly. Give me your coat.' And when she had passed it to him, 'Go into the drawing-room with Aunt Margaret. She has tea waiting for you.'

Laura drew a deep breath. 'Aren't you coming?' she asked fearfully.

'In a few minutes. Go with your aunt.'

'Yes.' But still she hesitated, thinking of the cheery warmth of her cottage and comparing it with this vast cold house whose very walls seemed to echo with ghostly whispers. Why had she been persuaded to come here? Why had she allowed Bren to talk her into accepting the post of companion to his aunt? But what alternative had she? There was nowhere for her to go, not unless she parted with her jewels—Laura Vernon's most treasured possessions. Bren had known all along that she would not let those go. And he had been generous, she supposed, in offering her a home in his house. Would she have accepted, though, had she not been in love with him? The answer to that was unimportant, for she *had* accepted, the temptation always to be near him being too great for her to resist. While she stood there, with these thoughts and questions running through her mind, she became aware of a shadowy figure drifting silently past Bren and out to the car. Uttering a little squeal, she made a grab at Bren's sleeve. 'Who's that?' she gasped.

'Feldon, my butler.' Bren uncurled her fingers from his coat. 'He's quite harmless; you'll get used to him.'

The drawing-room, where tea was ready on a table by the fire, had the same bleak and sombre aspect as the hall, and again a shudder passed through Laura as she stood for a moment looking round before taking the chair which the older woman was pulling out for her.

'Get yourself warm, dear. I'll pour you a nice cup of tea. The scones are freshly made, and here is the jam and cream.'

Scarcely conscious of the woman's words, Laura held out her hands to the fire, trying not to think of what she had lost. But her surroundings so filled her with dismay that she began again to wonder at her hasty acceptance of Bren's offer. His aunt had also called upon her at the cottage, and had been so charming and sympathetic. Then Bren called again, speaking to her quietly but in the same unmistakable tones of one whose habit it was to order. Her arguments that she had no idea of the duties of a lady's companion had been dismissed by the mere raising of his hand. She would soon learn, he had assured her, but in a way which seemed to imply that it was of no importance whether she learned the duties or not. Laura had given in almost eagerly at the end. For it was plain to see that she must leave her cottage, and had she been forced to leave the village as well, and never set eyes on Bren again, she felt her whole life would be finished.

Bren had seen to everything, even having gone to the extent of procuring a dealer to buy her few items of furniture and a man to take her poultry. And now here she was, living under the same roof as Bren, companion to his aunt. If only the house had been more pleasant and the atmosphere more warm and friendly she could perhaps in time have become reasonably happy in her new life. But the house—or what she had seen of it—terrified her, reminding her of ghosts and evil deeds. There was no love in it, no lingering echoes of children's laughter—and yet children had been born there—offspring of those wild Dewars whose headless ghosts still rode the deserted moorlands at dead of night. A deep sigh broke from Laura's lips. Her little cottage had always known love; the happiness and sorrow of Laura Vernon had consecrated it. Hate and malice had never defiled its walls. She sighed again, a troubled sigh, unaware that Bren had entered the room and was standing beside her chair, watching her bent head inscrutably.

'My dear child, whatever was that for?'

She glanced up, her eyes clouding.

'I was thinking of the cottage. When will the new people be moving in? I do hope it won't be long. Houses get lonely when they're left empty . . .' She stopped, feeling rather foolish as Bren drew an exasperated breath.

'You must try to forget it,' he advised her curtly. 'It's all in the past. You've a completely new future before you.' As he said that his eyes flickered automatically to his aunt's face, but naturally Laura attached no particular importance to the glance that passed between them.

'I'll never forget it,' she returned. 'And I shall never stop loving it.'

Aunt Margaret looked amazed. 'Love a cottage? What an extraordinary thing to say!'

'I told you I loved it, when you came to see me.'

'Oh yes,' admitted the older woman lightly. 'I gathered you liked living there—but to love four brick walls, and to say you'll always love them—it sounds quite absurd to me.'

'Most people love their homes,' Laura said with a touch of reproach.

'You're implying that we don't love ours?' said Bren with a sardonic twist of his lips.

'I wasn't ... well, I don't know.' Laura glanced round the room again. 'I'm sorry if I said anything to offend you.'

'I'm not so easily offended; perhaps it's because, unlike you, I'm not sentimental, either about my home or about people who've been connected with it.'

As soon as tea was over Laura was shown to her room. Standing on the threshold, she beheld the heavy furniture, the massive four-poster bed, the cold grey walls and drab curtains. It took a valiant effort to control her tears.

'It's very big,' she faltered, moving into the room as Aunt Margaret crossed over to draw the curtains.

'You'll find the whole place big, and strange, and perhaps a little overpowering at first after living in a tiny cottage, but you'll soon become used to it.'

Shivering in her great bed that night, Laura recalled those indifferently spoken words and, turning her head into the pillow, she wept bitter tears of loneliness and fear.

'I'll never become used to it, never! It's cold and horrid—and I'm beginning to think that all the people who live here are cold and horrid too!'

But she had not met Francis, who could be just as charming and friendly as his cousin was cold and impersonal. Although remarkably handsome, he did not carry his age well. He was thirty-one, two years younger than Bren, but looked at least five years older. He had the same dark eyes as Bren and the same black hair, and there the resemblance ended.

He put in an appearance the following day; Bren introduced him to Laura, watching them both closely as they shook hands. A moment later Laura was smiling up at Francis when something brought her eyes away from his. Bren and his aunt were looking at one another, Bren nodding almost imperceptibly and the woman responding, a look of intense satisfaction breaking over her dark and age-lined face.

CHAPTER THREE

FASCINATED and puzzled by this odd circumstance, Laura just stared. A frown darkened Bren's forehead as he realized she had noticed his aunt's somewhat triumphant expression.

'Come,' he snapped. 'The lunch is getting cold.'

'My fault,' apologized Francis. 'I felt off colour and couldn't decide whether or not to get up.'

A glance of contempt was his cousin's only reaction and had it been left to Bren the meal would have been eaten in complete silence. Francis, however, chatted all the time, mainly to Laura. Responding instantly to his charm, she talked to him without the least sign of shyness or hesitation. The meal over, Francis suggested a walk in the grounds; Laura glanced uncertainly at her employer.

'I shan't be needing you,' smiled Margaret. 'You're looking rather pale, dear, and a walk will do you good. Yes, by all means go along with Francis.'

'Thank you, Aunt Margaret.'

Laura's coat was in the hall, but Francis had to go upstairs for his and Laura waited for him outside the drawing-room, where Bren and his aunt were now sitting. The door stood half open and it was clear that they believed Laura and Francis to have gone because they talked freely, without even taking the precaution of lowering their voices.

'It should be easy,' Margaret was saying. 'But what about this William of whom you spoke? Is he going to interfere with our plans, do you think?'

'He could do. Has she been out with him this morning?'

Laura had to smile, even though dark frown lines

creased her brow. Bren obviously concluded that 'William' was her boy-friend, and had told his aunt about him. But what did the woman mean—it should be easy?

'No, she hasn't been out at all this morning. Incidentally, I must find her a few duties, otherwise she's going to ask herself why we've brought her here.'

'This William,' Bren remarked, ignoring his aunt's last words, 'she always sees him in the mornings—don't ask me why. He must be on night work or something, though where I can't imagine, for there's nowhere around here where he could be employed. However, from the entries in her diary it's clear that she sees him most mornings.'

'Well, she won't see him in the morning from now on,' Margaret declared emphatically. 'I'm not having some farm-labourer's son upsetting my plans.'

Laura heard no more. Francis was coming down the stairs and soon they were outside in the grounds, wandering past overgrown rose gardens and weed-ridden flower-beds. Her companion chatted, but Laura scarcely heard. Why had she been brought here?—to this dark and sinister abode where in the distant past the most fearsome deeds were perpetrated by those lawless men of Northumberland? Musing on the events leading up to her acceptance of the post of companion-maid to Lady Margaret, Laura recalled her firm but inexplicable conviction that even though Bren had suggested she sell some of her treasures and buy another house, he had instinctively known she would never dream of doing this. In fact, it was now very plain that, early in their acquaintanceship, Bren had decided she should come to live at the Abbey.

Why? she asked herself again, but although she continued to wrestle with the question, the reason for Bren's action still eluded her.

Her musings were brought to an abrupt end as

Francis chided her for not listening to him.

'I've been talking to myself for the past five minutes,' he complained, taking her arm as they reached a rough and stony path through what had once been a magnificent shrubbery. 'You never even heard my question, did you?' Laura bit her lip, flushing guiltily, and he added, 'I've just asked why I've never seen you before. What did you do with yourself? Didn't you ever go out?'

'I went for walks, yes, but mainly early in the morning, and in the evening. I like walking at dusk.' Her thoughts strayed again, this time to those occasions when she and her father would walk along the shore, in that twilight hour after sunset. They would cross the wet and gleaming sands until they reached the threshold of the sea. No harsh sounds to mar the silence—just the murmur of water rolling over the sands.

'That's why I haven't seen you. I'm never up in the morning,' admitted Francis with a grimace. 'And as for the evenings, I'm always otherwise occupied. Can't be bothered with too much walking, in any case. A saunter round the grounds like this is about my limit.'

'You'd love walking at dusk, with the wind in your face and the sound of surf in your ears. And you can see the Cheviots looking like great grey shadows against the sky, and if it's moonlight they seem to cut right into the fleecy little clouds which you so often see above the hills.'

He shook his head. 'I'm afraid I wouldn't like it at all. I'm no walker.'

'What do you do with yourself all day?' She glanced up at him curiously. Bren, she knew, worked hard on the estate, but Francis was something of a mystery figure. No one had ever seen him doing anything to help his cousin run this vast domain which included thousands of acres of hillside on which the famous Cheviot sheep freely grazed.

'Nothing in particular.' He laughed at her expression. 'I'm a gentleman of leisure.'

'Do you like that kind of life?' Laura hesitated before adding, 'Doing nothing all day, I mean?'

'I thoroughly enjoy it. Why work if you can possibly avoid it?'

Thinking about this for a space, Laura shook her head.

'It isn't good for a man—or a woman either—to do nothing, to have no interests.'

He glanced away and she missed his expression. Was there any truth in the rumour that he had bouts of insanity? It seemed impossible, she thought, looking at him now, noting his aristocratic profile and lordly bearing, and listening to his perfectly normal and intelligent conversation. And yet such cases were heard of from time to time, so she supposed there could be some foundation for the gossip concerning the heir to the title which was widely known to be proving so troublesome to his mother. Would she eventually get some girl to marry him? Laura wondered, recalling what Mr. Dodd had said about Lady Margaret's threat to marry Francis off to the gardener's daughter. Bren had not exactly said he would find a girl more suitable, but he *had* said he would have no country bumpkin's daughter in his house—and by that he meant, of course, the gardener's daughter.

As she and Francis continued their walk through the neglected grounds Laura transferred her thoughts to Bren. At what precise age had she discovered his attraction? Looking back, it seemed to Laura that she had always experienced a disturbing little jerk of her heart whenever she espied his tall figure in the distance. It was strange, but everyone else seemed to hold him in awe, repeating gruesome tales of his forebears, those heathen Northumbrians whose lust for barbaric devastation was notorious. Yes, it was most strange, mused

Laura, that all on the estate should regard Bren with this awe while she herself had long since lost her heart to him. What would be his reaction were he ever to learn of it? she wondered, a faint smile hovering on her lips. He would of course treat the whole thing with contempt, wondering how anyone could be so stupid as to have a crush on a man so very much her superior. Yes, she owned sadly, he would consider what she felt for him as nothing more important than a schoolgirl crush ... but Laura knew that her love for him went deep, so deep that nothing could ever weaken it, and no one else could ever take Bren's place in her heart.

Another strange thing was that she had never considered Bren to be her superior; always she was conscious of the relationship and the fact that, had fate not been so unkind, her great-grandmother would have occupied the exalted position of mistress of the Abbey.

They were back at the house before Laura even realized they had begun to retrace their steps. Bren and his aunt were still in the sitting-room and they both looked up as Laura entered, followed by Francis.

'Did you have a nice walk?' Margaret smiled at Laura and indicated a chair by the fire. 'You didn't stay out long.'

'I'd had enough.' Moving over to the sideboard, Francis picked up a whisky decanter, with the intention of pouring himself a drink. The cut-glass stopper was already out when, catching Bren's eye in the mirror, Francis replaced it in the decanter. Laura gasped. At one dark forbidding glance from his cousin Francis had meekly obeyed the unspoken command. 'Driving suits me better than walking,' said Francis sullenly, and took possession of a chair.

'Then you must take Laura for a drive,' suggested his mother. 'You'd like that, wouldn't you, dear?' She smiled at Laura, who made no reply. Her eyes were on

Francis, and his on her. For some reason she felt a tingling of apprehension and quickly transferred her gaze to Bren. There was a satisfied expression on his dark face, and yet a contradictory frown between his eyes. She might be naked, so interested was he in every line and curve of her body. Blushing at her thoughts, she lowered her head. But Bren's gaze remained on her; she could feel it and she stirred uncomfortably. What was there about these people that made them so different from everyone else? The Evil Dewars ... She thought of their fiendish ancestor, Red de Warre, great friend of another of the Conqueror's exalted vassals, the 'Wolf of Cheshire'. Merciless, both of them, torturers of their poor, helpless serfs, whose bodies would be slowly mutilated for the entertainment of their masters.

And these occupants of Fenstone Abbey were directly descended from Red de Warre; they carried his blood within their veins—and as for Bren, Laura could quite easily see him carrying many of Red's vices as well. For despite her great love for him, which she accepted even while vaguely wondering why she should love him, Laura had to own that his dark face quite often took on an evil aspect and she was sure that, had he lived in those barbaric ages long since past, he would also have derived enjoyment from the torture of those less fortunate than himself.

Barely two minutes passed before Francis was up again. Was it nerves that made him so fidgety? She had noticed it before, and usually it resulted in his having a full day in bed. When Laura had asked if she should go up and sit with him for a few minutes Bren had glared at her and told her abruptly that on no condition must she go up to Francis's bedroom. Francis moved about the room, rather like a caged lion, while Bren watched him contemptuously before once again allowing his eyes to examine every detail of Laura's figure. But he was thoughtful, and frowning heavily. With a swift abrupt movement he rose from his chair and left the room without a word.

The conversation between Margaret and her son was resumed and eventually Laura sat back in her chair, yawning as boredom swept over her. If only there were some fowls to attend to, or some cleaning up or baking to be done. As she yawned a second time Margaret stopped speaking and looked at her. She smiled sweetly—too sweetly, mused Laura with a frown—and said that, as she would not be requiring Laura's services that day, she could spend the rest of the afternoon doing whatever she wanted to do.

'Have a wander round the house,' she suggested. 'I want you to treat it as your home from now on . . . your permanent home, Laura dear.'

An odd significance was contained in those words, but although Laura experienced a tinge of uneasiness she deliberately cast it aside. Bren had brought her here and in spite of the conversation she had overheard between him and his aunt, Laura's trust in him was such that she had no difficulty in dismissing these slight misgivings. Bren would watch over her, and care for her. Wicked he might be, with bad blood in his veins, but she loved him, and with love came trust, complete and unquestioning.

The prospect of a gloomy exploration of the house being far from inviting, Laura made for the garden. The sun was shining; the air was clean and fresh, drenched with the tang of the sea, but the whole visual aspect was one of such neglect that she soon headed for the drive, leaving the grounds behind and traversing the lane fringed with gnarled old oaks and sombre pines. Down below was the wide sandy beach, backed by dunes. Despite the off-shore winds the waves rolled with white magnificence on to the beach, and in the far distance the lonely Farne Islands rose out of the sea—a disconnected part of the basaltic rocks of the Great Whin Sill. To the west were the undulating pastures of the Cheviot sheep, while further inland there rose the bastion of the Cheviot Hills proper, with the summit of the Cheviot itself lost in the clouds.

Laura caught her breath; the scenery was magnificent, the air like wine, the cry of the sea-birds like music to her ears. Her steps lightened as she walked along. Despite her firm assertion that she would never revisit the cottage she neared it automatically. But then she stopped, undecided. Unwise to proceed further; only a sort of nostalgic misery could result from a return to the place where she had known such happiness and deep contentment. The cottage could be seen, in its hillside setting with the peaty slopes on one side and the wild sea down below. Other scattered dwellings peeped through the trees or lay hidden by a rise, while to the north a glistening burn came rushing down to splash and tumble its way under the Old Bridge that spanned the village street.

Almost without conscious volition Laura made for the gate, but after long moments of indecision she gave a little shake of her head and retraced her steps. Nevertheless, the temptation to return was irresistible, and a week later she again reached the gate, this time passing through without hesitation into the garden, every inch of which had been tended by generations of loving hands.

No curtains yet ... how forlorn. And the garden had already taken on an aspect of neglect. Stooping, she pulled at some weeds which had invaded the herbaceous border. It was an all-absorbing task and the sound of a door opening went unheard as she stacked the weeds in the little pathway between the border and the tiny plot given over to roses. Wind caressed her hair, bringing disorder to her curls and an enchanting bloom to her cheeks. Straightening up at last, she gathered the weeds in her arms and carried them over to the compost heap at the side of the shed. The shed door was ajar and after depositing the weeds she peeped in. The floor was littered with paint cans, but only one caught her attention.

'Brown!' she exclaimed disgustedly. 'How unimaginative!'

'And what,' demanded a voice from behind, 'has that to do with you?'

She whipped round, her heart almost ceasing to beat as she eyed the frowning young man with consternation.

'I'm sorry...' She glanced past him to the open door of the living-room. 'I—I w-was just l-looking.'

His curious gaze took in her tousled hair, the rosy cheeks and the tremulous movement of her lips.

'Just looking, were you?' He glanced at the compost heap with its new addition of weeds. He was clearly both puzzled and surprised. 'Now why should you want to look, I wonder?' Laura said nothing and he added, a trifle sternly, 'You're trespassing.'

She winced, her eyes suddenly bright.

'I expect I am,' she agreed, twisting her hands in a little distracted gesture. The forlorn note in her voice brought a frown to his brow, but he waited, in an attitude of inquiry, expecting her to add to that brief admission, but she merely asked awkwardly, 'Are you the new tenant?' He was in overalls and his hands were smeared with paint—white paint.

'My brother is,' he informed her, and then, curiously, 'Who are you?'

'I live at the Abbey.' Involuntarily her hand was extended to indicate the dark silhouette high on the crags. 'Up there.' He glanced up at the house. 'You're not a Dewar.' It was a statement, and yet a question also, and Laura shook her head, smiling faintly.

'No, I'm a maid—a sort of companion as well—to

Lady Margaret.'

She cast another glance through the open door of the cottage. 'You appear to be very busy,' she added conversationally.

'I'm doing some decorating for my brother.' He paused, watching her closely. 'The place is in a dreadful state,' he added quietly, and evinced no surprise when her eyes opened wide and she said indignantly,

'What do you mean, in a dreadful state!'

An odd smile touched his lips. He's nice, Laura thought, and responded to his smile even though her indignation was still portrayed in her eyes.

'Come in and see for yourself.' He made a sweeping gesture towards the door.

Vigorously Laura shook her head.

'No—I mean—I won't waste your time.' She must not go in, strong as was the inclination to do so.

'My time's my own. Come on.' She still hesitated and he added as an inducement, 'I've just put the kettle on to make myself a cup of tea. You can have one if you like.'

Her smile deepened, and she hesitated no longer. They entered the living-room and in spite of her resolutions to be brave she felt the tears behind her eyes. What a mess! The floor was littered with paper which had been scraped off the walls; in one corner was what looked like a stack of firewood—— The shelves she and her father had made and fixed with such pride ... Her lip quivered and she turned away. By the window stood a pair of step-ladders.

'Don't you like the blue paint?' she inquired on a dry little sob, recalling how she had mixed the colour herself and then applied the paint with such care.

'My brother's wife chose the colours. She likes white for almost everything. The brown's for the shed,' he added with an unexpected smile of amusement, and she responded, although a trifle sheepishly. 'Come and see the sitting-room. Just look at that wall. Can you imagine anyone papering round a picture?'

Her pointed little chin lifted. 'Perhaps the picture had been there a—a hundred years!'

'At least a hundred, judging by the design on the paper underneath it.' He stared fixedly at the opposite wall, deliberately avoiding her gaze. For some reason Laura gained the impression that he was laughing to himself.

'There could have been some very good reason for not taking the portrait down—a sentimental reason, for instance.'

'Very true.' He turned then, his eyes twinkling. 'Now how did you know it was a portrait? I certainly didn't.' A flush spread over Laura's face and he added softly, 'Imagine your being like this.'

Her eyes flew to his. 'You know?'

'It was obvious from the start, wasn't it?'

She nodded, her glance straying through the window to where she had put the weeds on the compost heap.

'I expect it was.' She paused a moment. 'You've been teasing me.'

'I couldn't resist it.' He shook his head. 'Fancy a babe like you giving my brother all that trouble.'

A pained expression crossed her face and he instantly regretted his words.

'I didn't want to cause all that trouble. What did your brother think?'

He laughed, carried away by reflections.

'We all branded you a little vixen. What my mother said about you isn't repeatable. You see, my brother and his wife are living with Mum and Dad, but after the baby was born it was terribly inconvenient, because they had two children already. So Matthew applied for a job with a house. He was already working on the estate, but his particular job didn't carry a house.' He stopped, laughing again and regarding

Laura with that look of surprise and disbelief. 'The way we all called you—and you're not like that at all!'

Her face cleared. 'You don't think me a vixen now?'

'Most certainly not,' was the emphatic response. The kettle started whistling and he made for the kitchen, but at the door he turned. 'Wait till I tell them, they just won't believe it. You must come and see them just as soon as they move in.'

'When are they moving in?' she asked on his return. He carried a brown enamel teapot and two plastic beakers which he placed on the floor.

'When all the papering's finished. This is my trade,' he explained. 'I've a few days' holiday at present—saved them for the time when Matt and Lucy would be wanting the decorating done.' Bringing a wooden box from the corner, he placed it close to Laura. 'Have a seat. Sugar and milk?'

'Please.' Gingerly she sat down on the box, avoiding the rough splintered wood at the side.

'Good, because I've already put them in.' He poured the tea and handed her a beaker. 'My name's Don—Don Saunders. What's yours?'

'Laura Vernon.' She took the beaker; it was hot and she placed it on the floor.

'Laura Vernon . . . Hmm, I like Laura. Pleased to meet you. I hope the tea's to your liking.'

'I'm sure it will be. Thank you.' She felt shy, never before having been in the company of a young man in a situation like this. She had not felt shy with Francis, but then he was totally impersonal, whereas this young man was asking all sorts of questions, in addition to glancing at her now and then with what could only be described as admiration. 'How old are your brother's children?' she managed at length.

'Dodie's six, Lynn's five and the baby's called Kevin. He's just a year old.' Don's former surprise had faded and his regard was now one of interest. 'I had no idea

I'd meet with such good fortune when I came here today.' Don laughed at her blushes and she swiftly averted her head. He sat down among the paper shavings and continued to regard her.

'Your turn,' he said. 'Tell me how you came to be living here all alone, and how it was you took so long to move out?' He frowned slightly. 'Why are you up there at the Abbey? I live a few miles from here and don't hear the gossip, but Matt hears it, working on the Dewar estate, and he mentions them sometimes. A queer lot, from what I can make out.'

Laura smiled faintly at his description of them, and after a moment she began to talk, naturally omitting details of the past, but telling Don of her father's death and her own reluctance to leave the cottage in which she had been born. His face softened before she had gone very far; she noticed the compassion in his eyes and knew for sure that she liked this young man whom she had so unexpectedly encountered on entering the garden.

'What tough luck! You sound as if you're extraordinarily attached to the place.'

'I am. You see, we had it for generations.' Laura almost added that she had offered to buy it, but checked herself, unwilling to mention Laura Vernon's jewels.

'These big estate owners usually want their houses for their employees,' commented Don a trifle apologetically.

'Yes, I know . . . only Father had worked on the estate since he was a boy of fifteen and I did think Mr. Dewar would have let me stay, but he wouldn't.'

'That would be the cousin? Bren, I think they call him?'

'Yes, that's right.'

'He's a most formidable man, so I'm told?'

Laura glanced through the window. There was a

mysterious quality about Fenstone Abbey in this grey haze of approaching dusk. Its shape cut grotesquely into the sky, and a pair of peregrine falcons planing and diving above the crumbling tower were merely dark smudges with neither colour nor shape discernible.

'They are a strange family altogether,' she admitted reluctantly at last, bringing her gaze back to her companion. 'And, as you say, Bren is formidable—at least, to other people.'

Her last words registered and the touch of a frown creased his brow. However, all he said was,

'How do you come to be working up there?'

'They offered me the post and I had no alternative but to accept it—not really.'

'How very odd...' Don spoke to himself and she saw his lips purse as he fell silent, deep in thought. 'The post vacant ... just at the time you were in need of somewhere to go.'

'I don't think Lady Margaret had a companion before,' said Laura innocently, and at that the young man looked sharply at her.

'The post was created, then—especially for you?'

She blinked. The idea had naturally crossed her mind, but now she came to dwell on it she experienced again that inexplicable tinge of uneasiness. Why should they create a post especially for her? It wasn't as if they were the types who would go out of their way to be kind and understanding. They had never been known to help anyone or even to subscribe to any of the village charities.

'I suppose it was created just for me,' she admitted as Don sat there, looking interrogatively at her. 'I'm all right, though,' she hastened to say on perceiving the anxiety in his eyes. 'Lady Margaret's very kind.'

'But the son—it's said he's an imbecile——'

'Don't say such a word!' she cut in, throwing him an

indignant glance. 'He has funny turns—so it's said by people in the village—although my father never agreed about this, saying there was nothing seriously wrong with Francis.'

'There are always foundations for rumours. From what I've heard he's sometimes put in a special room.'

Laura had also heard this and she fell silent, thinking of the vastness of the house and the numerous closed doors, most of which led off a maze of corridors, draughty and dark. Could there be such a room behind one of those closed doors? Take a look round the house, Aunt Margaret had said ... Laura determined to do just that.

'He seems quite normal to me,' she commented, looking at Don. 'But I suppose there could be such a room and he could have this illness of which people sometimes speak.'

'I feel pretty certain he has this illness, as you call it. Make sure you're not around when he has one of his attacks.'

'Francis would never hurt me,' returned Laura with confidence.

'You can't say what he'd do if he weren't in full possession of his senses. People like that aren't responsible for their actions.' Picking up his beaker, he took a drink, continuing to hold the cup to his lips as he became lost in thought, and while he was thus absorbed Laura was able to take a good look at him. A strong face, but boyish. Light brown hair and a frank open expression. Inexplicably she was glad she had met him.

Later, he accompanied her up the hill and on saying goodbye he extended an eager invitation for her to come again, the following day if possible.

She hesitated, but not for long.

'All right, I'll come tomorrow. It will be in the afternoon, as it was today.'

'Fine. I'll work hard during the morning and shan't feel guilty at taking an hour off to entertain you.' His ready smile flashed as he turned away. In a little while Laura twisted round and a lightness entered her heart as she saw that he was looking back. They waved to one another until Don was lost to sight round a bend in the lane.

She had been away more than two hours and Bren met her as she entered the hall. His keen dark eyes searched her face before he said abruptly.

'Where have you been? Aunt Margaret's been looking for you.'

For some reason she could not define Laura was unable to mention her visit to the cottage and the meeting with Don.

'Only for a walk,' she evaded, refusing to meet his gaze.

'A walk? Where to?'

'Along the lanes—and into the village—— Well, almost into the village,' she amended, her conscience assuaged by the fact that it was only a white lie. Bren continued his searching scrutiny; she felt he intended to learn more, and with a swift sideways movement she slid past him and ran upstairs to her room.

CHAPTER FOUR

THE following afternoon Laura was again at the cottage, drinking tea and chatting to Don. He had worked hard since she left him yesterday and not only was the painting in the living-room finished, but the wall-papering was well on its way to completion. Laura felt cheered by this transformation and had to admit, on being questioned, that it was an improvement on the way she had had it herself.

'You're an expert, though,' she smiled. 'Father and I were not very good at decorating.'

'Thanks for the compliment.' He spoke teasingly, but there was also a seriousness about him which greatly appealed to Laura. Never until this moment had she fully realized just how lonely and lost she had felt since the death of her father, but now her position hit her forcibly. What were her prospects of a happy life?—of knowing the fulfilment of marriage and a home and children? She would never marry, she told Mr. Dodd, and meant it. How was marriage possible when she so deeply loved a man who would never look at her in that sort of way? Bren had never looked at any woman—so it was said—and if this were true it was well beyond the bounds of possibility that he would ever look at her, considering her to be no more than a child, as his manner towards her unquestionably proved. No, there were no happy prospects of marriage and children for her, so she might as well not think about the future at all.

Yet as she sat there with Don a strange new contentment gradually took possession of her, and when, after he had washed the beakers, and she had dried them, he suggested a walk, she readily agreed, although she did say she must not keep him too long from his work.

'I'll pull up,' he said unconcernedly, and then went on in puzzled tones, 'How is it that you can get out like this? Surely you don't have every afternoon off?'

She hesitated, recalling their previous discussion about the post having been made especially for her.

'I haven't really started work yet,' she admitted. 'I think Lady Margaret will be finding me something to do shortly.' Reaching the gate, she pushed it open before he could do so. 'I expect you find it strange,' she said on noticing his frown.

'Damned strange! If they offered you a job, then they should automatically give you duties to perform.'

She nodded. 'Yes, that's what I think.' He was anxious about her and she liked it. It was a new experience and a pleasant one and suddenly she found herself confiding in him, repeating what she had overheard in the conversation between Lady Margaret and her nephew.

'She said those things?' Don's frown was now a scowl.

'Yes, truly. She said she must find me a few duties soon or I would be asking myself why they had taken me to the Abbey.'

She and Don were strolling towards the shore and the wind blew strongly against them, slowing down their progress. Don took her arm and she found a shyness creeping over her at the close contact with another human being. But she did not draw away and they walked some distance in silence, each absorbed in thought. He was very nice indeed, thought Laura, and hoped the friendship would continue.

'There's something more than a little mysterious about the whole business,' said Don emphatically at last. 'Why should they concern themselves about you at all? It isn't as if they have any sort of reputation for concerning themselves with others in this sort of way.

It's decidedly fishy—could almost be some sort of conspiracy.'

'Conspiracy?' Laura turned her head to stare at him. 'I don't know what you mean?'

'I don't know, either,' was the grim response. 'All I do know is that the Dewars are acting in a way totally out of character, and I'm suspicious. I was talking to my brother about it last night——'

'You told your brother about me?'

'Only in a casual way,' he replied quickly. 'I said you'd been to the cottage and we'd been chatting—he and Mum were quite amazed when I told them how nice you are,' he said, veering the subject for the moment. 'But I convinced them and they want to see you. Mum says I must take you home—when Matt and Lucy have moved, because it tends to be bedlam at present—with the overcrowding, and the three youngsters rarely quiet for a moment.' He paused for a while and they stopped to watch the rollers breaking on the shore. 'As I was saying,' he continued when they were on their way again, 'I spoke about you—and your job up at the Abbey—to Matt, and he also expressed his puzzlement and disbelief at this help they appear to be giving you.' Don turned his head and she saw the anxiety in his eyes. 'We've known each other only a few hours in all,' he said, 'but I want you to know you have a friend, Laura, a friend you can trust, and who will be right there to help should the need for help ever arise. Understand?' So grave was his tone, and deeply expressive, and she was suddenly encompassed by a feeling of security and warmth. No longer was she alone, and friendless. Yet she spoke quite unconcernedly when she replied, for she never thought for one moment that she would ever require the help he was offering.

'Yes, I understand.' And after a rather shy hesitation she added, 'I think you're a very kind person, Don.' The name slipped hesitantly from her lips, and she liked the sound of it. 'I'm glad you want to be my friend.' Don stopped and faced her; her beautiful eyes looked into his, shyly but not unwillingly. She was entering upon a new experience, one that bewildered but in no way excited her. 'I haven't ever had a friend before.'

The truth shocked him.

'Not even a girl friend?—a companion to go about with?'

'No, only my father. We were everything to one another and neither of us needed anyone else.'

'We all need friends, Laura.' He sounded deeply concerned. 'Have you no relatives at all—not even a distant cousin or aunt?'

'No one.' But she smiled, and a soft flush of pleasure rose to enhance her beauty. 'I have a friend now, though,' she murmured, wishing they would walk on again so that Don could take her arm, as he had done before.

'You have a friend,' he echoed fervently. 'Always remember that.' They did walk on, and he did take her arm, tucking it into his. 'You'll have other friends when my brother and his wife move into the cottage. Do you like kids?'

'I haven't had much to do with them,' she answered regretfully. 'But I think I like them.' Don laughed at that but made no comment. 'Will you be living at the cottage?' she asked then, and he said no, but he would be a regular visitor.

'In any case,' he added, 'you'll be coming to see my mum and dad. You can come on Sundays for tea.'

'I might not be able to get out on Sundays.'

'You're doing very well up till now. In any case, even if you are given duties to perform you'll most likely have Sundays off.'

'It would be nice to go out to tea,' she murmured, almost to herself. She had never in the whole of her life been a guest in anyone's house and the idea of visiting Don's parents was something to which she would look forward. 'When will your brother and his family be moving in?' she asked, her thoughts switching to the cottage again. She had asked the same question yesterday, she recalled, but before she had time to say anything he was answering.

'I'm hoping to have the place ready in about a fortnight. Of course, I go back to work on Monday, so there'll only be the evenings and week-ends, but I should get it done; the place is really quite small.'

They continued along the sands for a little while longer, but the wind began to blow cold and they decided to turn back.

'Shall I come again tomorrow?' she asked shyly as she left him at the cottage gate.

'Of course. I shall be very disappointed if you don't.'

On her way back Laura decided to make a small detour and call in at Mr. Dodd's cottage. He was sitting by the fire, listening to the radio when she tapped on the window and asked if she could come in.

'Yes, young Laura. Come on in, by all means.' She went round to the back door and a moment later she was sitting opposite to him, warming her hands by the fire. 'It's healthy you're looking, young Laura. Life up at the big house must be agreeing with you.'

She made no comment on that remark, merely inquiring about his wife.

'Still the same. Aches and pains, and can't move most of the time. Go on up if you like; she'll be glad of a visitor.'

'Yes, I will go up.' Rising again, Laura made for the narrow stairs and ran lightly up them. Mrs. Dodd looked much older than her sixty-two years and Laura wondered why people had to suffer such pain as they grew older. She remembered Mrs. Dodd years ago, when she was so sprightly that she could go out into

Alnwick and work in offices there, as well as looking after her own house and husband. But now she was tied to her bed for most of the time, although she valiantly did get up on occasions and try to get about and do some chores in the house. She smiled at Laura and patted the bed, inviting her to sit down.

'You're up at the Abbey, I hear,' she said. 'Tell me all about it. Are you really companion-maid to Lady Margaret?'

'Yes—well, that's what I shall be, but I haven't started work yet.'

'Funny, them taking you. Not at all like the Dewars to think of anyone but themselves. They must be reforming in their old age——' She broke off, uttering a groan and moving about in the bed, as if trying to find a comfortable position.

'Are you in very dreadful pain?' asked Laura awkwardly. She never quite knew what to say to Mrs. Dodd. It seemed wrong to inquire about her pain, and equally wrong to refrain from asking about it.

'One of my bad days, dear. Rain's about, and that makes it very much worse.'

They talked for a little while, but Laura could see that Mrs. Dodd was becoming tired and she bade her good afternoon and left the room.

'There's a cup of tea for you,' said Mr. Dodd when she came down again. 'Has Mrs. Dodd been gossiping?'

'Gossiping? No. What would she gossip about?'

'So long as she hasn't we'll let the matter drop, young Laura. Put some sugar in your tea, and have a biscuit with it. You'll find one in the tin over there on the sideboard.'

'I don't want anything to eat, thank you, Mr. Dodd.' Laura sat down and took her cup and saucer from the table in front of her. Gossip ... Why ask if his wife had been gossiping and then abruptly refuse to carry the conversation further? Laura sipped her tea, dismissing the tiresome question of the gossip. People were probably talking about her job up at the Abbey; it was a nine-days' wonder and would be forgotten the moment something more interesting cropped up, such as a birth or death in the village.

'What's it like, living in the grand style?' asked Mr. Dodd, taking out his pipe and lighting it. 'I said as you was a bit uppish, if you remember. Sort of thinking yourself the aristocracy, as it were. Well, now you're living in a fine house you should be feeling quite at home.' He puffed at his pipe but regarded her through the cloud of smoke, an odd expression on his face.

'You did say I was—er—haughty,' she agreed, her colour rising slightly. 'And I said I wasn't.'

'You are, though. The village lads aren't good enough for you; you said.'

'No, I didn't! I merely said I didn't want to go a-courting with one of the boys from the estate.'

'And that was because you were liking someone much higher up, young Laura.' He smiled at her through the smoke. 'It's a funny business altogether, and I'm a-thinking someone's going to be very disappointed when all the cards are thrown on the table.'

She stirred impatiently. 'You talk in riddles, Mr. Dodd.'

'Maybe ... but I can't explain. Watch yourself, though, young Laura. I likes you and I think you can take care of yourself if anything happens——'

'Mr. Dodd, what do you mean?' Laura spoke with unaccustomed sharpness, because, much to her surprise, her nerves were very much on edge. All these hints and warnings. What could they mean? First Don and now Mr. Dodd. Then there was the gossip he mentioned and which she, Laura, had so lightly dismissed, believing she knew what it was all about. But did she know what it was all about?'

'Have I scared you? I'm sorry, then. But as I was a-saying, I think you can take care of yourself, but watch what goes on for all that. Those Dewars are as evil now as when they were murdering their neighbours and throwing their heads into the river.'

Her impatience grew; finishing her tea, she put the cup and saucer on the table and rose from her chair.

'I must be going,' she said. 'Good afternoon, Mr. Dodd. I hope Mrs. Dodd will be feeling better tomorrow.'

'Maybe she will and maybe she won't. Good afternoon, young Laura. Thanks for dropping in ... and mind what I said to you.'

Try as she would Laura could not now dismiss her tinglings of apprehension. And yet what could possibly happen to her? Bren was there ... Her sweet young mouth curved tenderly. What had she to worry about while Bren was there? Hadn't she told herself he could be trusted to take care of her? Of course he would take care of her...

On her return she saw Bren standing by the edge of the lake, his hands thrust deeply into his pockets, his features grim and gaunt in the shadows of an overhanging willow tree. The sides of the lake were a tangle of rotting vegetation; its surface was coated with thick green slime and putrid water-weed. Close by several lichen-covered statues gave evidence of a bygone splendour, but now everything wore a bleak and sinister aspect, in conformity with the grey, ivy-strangled house clinging to the ragged cliffs.

Laura halted some small distance from Bren. Austere he looked, and formidably autocratic, his dark head arrogantly tilted as, turning smoothly, he allowed his eyes to rove over her from head to foot before finally coming to rest on her face.

'You've been out a long while,' he commented, watching her closely.

'Have I?' She played for time, although she had not the least idea why she should. This obviously wasn't the response he desired, for his eyes narrowed and an arrogant note edged his voice when he spoke.

'Three hours, to be exact.' Laura merely swallowed hard, and he added with soft deliberation, 'Where have you been?'

'Walking,' she told him after a small hesitation.

'That's the answer you gave me yesterday.' A thoughtful pause and then, 'Three hours is a long time to walk about ... alone?' This was a subtle question; Laura swallowed again and her face paled slightly. Why this reluctance to be open, to say naturally and casually that she had been to the cottage and had been walking with Don? After all, she was not obliged to account to Bren for her time. 'I asked you a question, Laura.' So soft his tones, yet sinister—or so it seemed to Laura.

'I wasn't alone.' She met his stare, but added nothing to that simple admission, for she was afraid, somehow, and her heart pulsated most unnaturally.

Bren's eyes kindled.

'You were not alone? Then whom were you with?'

Instinctively her chin tilted despite her tinge of fear. And her proud eyes flashed and widened to an incredible size.

'I went to the cottage,' she informed him. 'A young man—the brother of the man who is going to live there—was decorating. He walked part of the way back with me.'

He measured her darkly, arrogance in every chiselled line of his face. Laura began to regret her little spurt of militance.

'You talked—and walked—with a complete stranger?' She did not reply and he added, 'Was this man a stranger, or had you met him before?'

Laura nodded, and stared with concentration at her

hands, clasped tightly in front of her. Fear increased, but anger rose too, because she ought not to be afraid.

'I met him yesterday.' Laura ventured a glance from under long dark lashes. Bren's displeasure was marked. 'You yourself suggested I go back and have a look at the cottage,' she then reminded him rather hastily. 'Don was there and he asked me in. He gave me a cup of tea,' she added irrelevantly.

'So you were not walking yesterday—not all the time.' Hard eyes bored into her. 'You lied to me, in fact.'

A soft flush of colour highlighted the noble contours of her face.

'Not exactly—I mean, I omitted to mention Don, of course——'

'Deliberately, I take it. Why?'

A little lump settled in her throat, the product both of anger and of fear. Her voice became slightly high-pitched owing to these emotions.

'I don't know,' she answered truthfully. 'I suppose I felt you wouldn't approve of my making friends with Don.'

Silence fell between them, but from the distance drifted the music of a peaty burn cascading down from ledge to ledge in a series of rapids, or tiny waterfalls.

'This Don—he's the brother, you say, of Matthew Saunders?' When at last Bren spoke his voice was tinged with anger, a circumstance which added strength to her assumption that he would not approve of her friendship with Don.

'That's right. Don's a decorator by trade and he's had a few days' holiday in order to do the house up for Matthew.'

His eyes flickered to her face, but then his expression became veiled.

'You appear to have struck up a firm friendship with this Don ... in a very short time,' he murmured, softly yet somehow dangerously, and Laura swallowed, trying to dislodge the obstruction in her throat.

'I hope he will be my friend,' she returned defiantly. 'I've never had a friend before.'

It was a matter-of-fact statement, but Laura eyed Bren expectantly, seeking for some sign of understanding, but his features retained their harsh and merciless lines. His thin lips were tight, his eyes as dark and hard as obsidian. An obscure unfathomable emotion possessed her like some fleeting dream; she was searching, yearning and even hoping ... but for what? She closed her eyes, wondering what it would be like to be in this man's arms, to have those cruel lips pressed ruthlessly on to hers, to have him pick her up and ride away with her as so many of his wild ancestors had ridden away with their neighbours' wives or daughters.

Laura opened her eyes, flushing at her thoughts. Bren noted this fluctuating colour and his black brows lifted a fraction, questioningly. Laura averted her head. Her long dark hair fell forward like a shining silken cloak about her shoulders. With a timid fawn-like swing of her lovely body she took her weight from one foot to the other, a movement which brought her a step nearer to her formidable companion.

She looked up; his expression was unreadable.

'Today,' he said at length, 'how long were you at the cottage?'

She frowned, and Bren's gaze narrowed in a rather ominous way. 'I suppose I was there about an hour, and then we went for the walk.' Laura's eyes were drawn to the window of the sitting-room. Margaret was standing there looking out at them with an almost scowling expression on her face. Arrested, Bren turned his head. A sneer twisted the thin lips unpleasantly before Bren turned again, giving his attention once more to Laura.

'An hour, eh? What were you doing during that

time?'

'We had a cup of tea—and talked.'

He looked down at her from his great height. 'What about?'

She frowned again, but avoided his gaze. 'All sorts of things.'

'Such as?'

His persistence annoyed her, but because she was strangely happy in Bren's company she let her anger die and gave him a smile. His face remained unsmiling, although she felt sure she detected a flicker of interest in his eyes.

'It was about the house, mainly—at that time.'

'What do you mean, at that time?' he asked, and she bit her lip. She should have been more guarded.

'When we were out walking we talked about my job,' she told him after a long and thoughtful moment of indecision during which she reached the conclusion that he would persist until she had acquainted him with every single thing she had said and done.

'Your job?' sharply. 'You discussed your job with this young man?'

She met his gaze and noted the strangeness there—in fact it was suddenly borne in on her that Bren's whole manner was extraordinarily peculiar.

'We talked about my coming up here, yes. I said of course that I hadn't started yet——'

'You told him you hadn't started?' he interrupted almost harshly.

'It was the truth,' she pointed out, acutely aware of his simmering wrath. But, strangely, she sensed it was not against her but against his aunt, for instinctively he turned his head in the direction of the window again and although Margaret was no longer there Bren's mouth went tight and his dark eyes smouldered dangerously. When he twisted round again he said, abruptly changing the subject,

'Laura, have you a young man—a young man you've been going out with, I mean?'

Her eyes flew to his; it was clear he was thinking of 'William'. Yet his interest puzzled her, for both he and his aunt seemed to be troubled by the fact that she might have a boy-friend. Something made her say,

'If that were the case wouldn't he have come to my assistance when I was having to leave the cottage?'

Bren's eyes kindled dangerously.

'Laura,' he said gently, 'I don't tolerate impertinence—from anyone. So I advise you to take care.' Her colour mounted; he watched it in silence for a long moment before he said, in the same soft unhurried tones, 'I noticed when I visited you at the cottage that you were writing about someone called William. Who is he?'

She paused in thought. There was no doubt at all that William was causing some considerable anxiety, and again she wondered why. For the present, though, she must think up some plausible answer to give him. But although she searched frantically nothing came to mind, and when at last he gave an impatient sigh she told him apologetically that she could not speak of William.

'It's a private matter,' she added rather lamely, feeling dejected at the idea of Bren's believing she had a boy-friend. But she could scarcely acquaint him with the truth and inform him that he himself was William. He regarded her inscrutably and for a while the noise of the tumbling burn was the only break in the silence. And then, suddenly, his eyes widened with perception and a strange smile touched the corners of his mouth. Had he guessed? she wondered, going slightly pink. As the silent moments passed and she read a dawning amusement in those hard eyes she knew he had reached some conclusion ... but she was strangely convinced that it was far from being the correct one. He said no more about the matter, and after casually mentioning that her duties would begin the following morning he swung about and strode briskly away in the direction of the house.

Tea was a quiet meal, with tension in the air. Margaret would often glare balefully at Bren, while he himself sat in thought, scarcely eating at all as his eyes wandered now and then to Francis and then to Laura. She watched him, and wondered . . . Don had said there was something decidedly fishy about the Dewars' action in bringing her up to the Abbey, and Mr. Dodd had declared it to be 'a funny business altogether', and had gone on to advise her to watch herself. What did it all mean? Certainly there was some mystery about her being here, and with this conviction came a tingling of apprehension even while she knew deep down in her heart that she had nothing to fear because Bren was there. Yet she had to face the fact that he was deeply involved in whatever mystery surrounded her presence in this great house. He it was who persuaded her to come—after firmly refusing to let her retain the tenancy of the cottage. He personally had assisted her to move, an act which only now did she see was far beneath his dignity. It was almost as if he feared she might elude him—slip away somewhere to a place where she could not be found. His aunt too had been so charming and persuasive, while Laura in her innocence and trust had been filled with gratitude even though she was at that time steeped in sadness and misery at the thought of leaving her home. These reflections occupied her mind all through tea, for no one spoke to her, even Francis being lost in thought. The meal over Laura was quick to make her escape, and as she silently left the room her last impression was that both Bren and his aunt were now only waiting for Francis to make a similar move so that they could get at each other's throats.

Once on the wide circular landing Laura stopped to peer over the heavy oak balustrade to the floor below. No sign of anyone coming out of the sitting-room ... She trod cautiously and silently, making for the west wing, a part of the Abbey which Margaret had said was never used now and so there was nothing to see, most of the rooms being empty. The first door gave way, creaking under the slight push of her hand. Empty, as Margaret had said. The next room was locked; bending down, Laura looked through the keyhole. A few massive pieces of furniture and nothing else. A third room sent shivers up her spine. The floor was carpeted with dust and grime, the paper drooped from high damp walls. The smell of must almost suffocated her and from the towering ceiling cobwebs hung by the hundred. She closed the door and stood with her hand on the ornate brass knob, dwelling on the past splendour of the place and the balls and parties which would be held there in the glittering days of William, the man who had desired to make Laura Vernon his wife.

A sound from below brought her away from the door and she peered once more into the hall. Francis was coming out of the sitting-room; he amazed her by acting as cautiously and as stealthily as she. First, he actually tiptoed to the front door, then changed his mind and moved noiselessly to a small side door, and was just about to pass through it when he glanced up and saw Laura. Sheepishly he grinned at her, hesitated uncertainly and then disappeared without troubling to close the door behind him. What could he be up to? she wondered. His stealthy secretive behaviour contributed to the mystery and she sped down the stairs with the intention of following him, when raised voices from the sitting-room arrested her. She paused in indecision, glancing from one door to the other. Francis had a start on her, so she might have lost him already, she decided. And in any case it was not a good idea of hers to follow him because unless he went through the wooded part of the grounds she would have no cover and he would see her at once. And so she cautiously moved to the sitting-room door, experiencing no qualms regarding the deliberate intention to eavesdrop as she stood by the slightly open door. There was a mystery and she intended solving it if she could.

'— all this talk about my not giving her some work to do when you yourself aren't helping by walking with her in the garden!' Lady Margaret's voice was high-pitched with anger. Bren's on the other hand was softly controlled as he said,

'What exactly does that imply?'

'It doesn't imply anything. It's a warning. We don't want any complications. We don't want her falling in love with *you*!' Great stress was laid on the last word, but the speaker was so angry that Laura couldn't have said if the stress was by accident or design. The words were puzzling, nevertheless, and Laura was frowning heavily as she endeavoured to discover some reason for them when Bren's laugh drove everything else from her mind. It was low, yet harsh and satanic and totally devoid of humour.

'So that was why you were scowling at me through the window?' His laugh vibrated again and a shudder passed through Laura in spite of her love for the man. He was wicked. Wickedness was demonstrated in that terrible sound. Contained in it was every conceivable measure of ruthlessness and cruelty. Such would have been the laugh of his ancestors as they sat in splendour on the green, witnessing the blinding, or the cutting off of the ears of one of their serfs as punishment for some minor crime committed in desperation with hunger as the cause.

'Do you honestly believe there's any likelihood of

that?' exclaimed Bren when he had recovered. 'You underrate the child's intelligence!'

Laura winced as a stab of pain tore at her heart.

'One woman fell in love with you, Bren——' Margaret's voice had lost its wrathful edge but acquired a sneering quality which grated on Laura's ears. 'Or have you forgotten? It must be ... let me see ...' A silence fell while she mentally calculated. 'You were twenty at the time, so it's eleven years since your romantic little affair with Rita MacShane.'

Another silence. A tenseness enveloped Laura's body. The waiting seemed interminable before Bren spoke.

'You call that love?' So harsh the tone, yet vibrantly acrid. 'The fair Rita prudently heeded the advice of her parents, if you remember, and fought shy of marrying a Dewar.'

Laura's nerves fluttered. She should not be listening to a conversation such as this. She had only desired to learn something which would contribute to the solving of the mystery—but now she had heard of this Rita she could not drag herself away from the door.

'She married someone else, yes, but everyone knew she was in love with you.' The sneer remained, though less pronounced. 'How long has she been a widow?'

'A widow...' Laura raised a hand to her mouth, fearful lest her utterance had been heard inside the room. But she breathed freely again as Bren began to speak.

'Almost a year.' Indifference now in his voice. Was it assumed?—merely for his aunt's benefit? Was he still in love with this Rita? Laura had never even visualized having Bren herself—she knew it was quite impossible—but she felt she could live quite comfortably so long as he never had anyone else. If he were ever to marry she felt she would die.

'A year,' repeated Margaret thoughtfully. 'Long

enough for mourning these days. She'll be in circulation again by now. You should do a little investigating, Bren; you might find she still has a hankering to be dominated and crushed by the most devilish of all the Dewars.'

'All?' echoed Bren calmly, ignoring the rest of Margaret's little speech.

'There are only us left, I know that, but I applied the adjective to all the Dewars that have ever been.' The sneer was very pronounced now, and again the evil laugh rang out before Bren said,

'I believe there have been worse than I.'

'Only because barbaric deeds are not now permitted. If they were you'd devise tortures which would far surpass any used by your forebears.'

'You're insinuating that I'm living out of my age?' queried Bren with a short mirthless laugh.

'Exactly. You're completely out of place in this day and age.'

'Then that makes two of us,' came the swift and sardonic retort from Bren.

'Let's get back to practicalities,' she snapped. 'The first thing is for you to keep her at a distance.'

'You're speaking of Laura, I presume?'

Laura's heartbeats quickened. What was the meaning of all this?

'Secondly,' said Margaret, ignoring his question, 'these duties you're so troubled about. I'll find her something to do, as you said. She can busy herself in my bedroom.'

'How you propose to employ her is your own affair,' said Bren in tones of bored impatience, 'but see that she is employed—at once.'

'This boy you spoke of,' said Margaret after a pause, 'he's not William, you say?'

'Do I have to repeat everything?' he snapped. 'No, William is not the boy she sees at the cottage. In fact,

I've come to the conclusion that William is non-existent.'

Laura caught her breath, waiting. This then was the conclusion he had reached, out there in the garden.

'He's non-existent? What are you talking about?'

'He's the man in the portrait—William Dewar, her great-grandmother's lover. The girl's associated herself romantically with the first Laura Vernon. She's been lonely since the death of her father and she's played this little game of make-believe as a diversion.'

'You're sure?'

'Almost sure, yes.'

'The stupid creature!'

A glint of steel brightened Laura's eyes and her small fists clenched.

'You think so?' came the surprising response. 'But then you wouldn't understand, would you?'

'I don't know what you mean?'

'And I haven't the patience to explain—nor have I the patience to stay here. You bore me to distraction.'

'Then why don't you get out!'

'And leave my home?'

'It should be mine!'

'So it should,' sneered Bren. 'Perhaps I will get out one of these days—and if I happen to be in a generous mood I'll make this—er—stately pile over to you and your charming son.'

'And the money?' put in his aunt eagerly.

'Greed was always one of your deplorable number of vices,' he sneered. 'No, I'll not give you money to send after the other. In any case, it's rightfully mine——'

'*My* husband left it to you!'

'And *my* grandfather left it to him. It's rightfully mine,' he repeated with stress and deliberation.

At the sudden scraping of a chair being slid back Laura sped away, making for the stairs, which she took with the swiftness and grace of a doe, and she was well out of Bren's vision when a moment later he emerged from the sitting-room and closed the door quietly behind him.

After making sure he was not intending to come upstairs Laura continued her exploration of the rooms in the west wing, although her mind was fully occupied with what she had overheard. How they hated one another, those two! They could not even make an attempt at civility. Would Bren go away? she wondered, a rush of dejection sweeping over her for a space. No, it was only a half-hearted threat, and an equally half-hearted promise. Bren would never give his aunt the satisfaction of owning the Abbey, Laura told herself, casting off her dejection. Laura's thoughts turned once again to Rita and instantly another casting off took place. She was by nature of a happy disposition and she had no intention of dwelling on the possibility of a marriage between Bren and this girl he had known all those years ago. Time enough to upset herself if ever they should meet and appear to be taking up the threads of that long-past romance. What did disturb Laura was that particular emphasis Margaret had used when she said,

'We don't want her falling in love with *you*!'

There seemed no sense in the utterance—and yet Bren appeared to catch on to its meaning. Laura shrugged impatiently as she entered yet another room. The mystery would appear to be deepening all the while and she wondered if it would ever be solved.

The room she entered was in a filthy condition, festooned with cobwebs and rank with mildew and must. Moving to the other side, she stood by the window, scarcely able to see out owing both to the masking ivy growing over it and the actual grime on the window itself. The curtains hung, rotting and heavy with dust, from the enormous brass rail under an oaken pelmet.

Laura shuddered and, making for the door, stepped out on to the landing. Two more rooms in this part of the house and then she must begin on another wing. Alert, she listened, but no sound assailed her ears and she opened yet another door. Unlike the rest it swung smoothly inwards on well-oiled hinges. Laura paused on the threshold, staring. Her mouth became dry, her hand on the door knob felt icy cold. The windows had been blocked out, but light slanted through a skylight high in the roof; the walls and floor were padded, as was the low seat fastened to one wall.

As if drawn by some magnetic force she entered the room, snapping on a light as she did so. The floor was soft beneath her feet; it seemed unreal. Reaching out gingerly, as if about to test something hot, she pushed one finger against the wall. The very feel of it was revolting——

Her spine tingled and she spun round. Someone was coming up the stairs—so very quietly. On sudden impulse she pushed the door to, glancing up at the skylight and noticing with relief that it was slightly open. She took a deep breath, endeavouring to relieve the suffocating sensation that assailed her chest and throat. The quiet footsteps stopped; the door was closed sharply and Laura's heart leapt into her throat as she heard the insertion of a key into the lock. Flinging herself at the door, she tried to wrench it open, uttering a strangled little scream as she did so. The key was turned again and the door swung inwards.

'You . . .!' White to the lips, Laura stared at the thin-faced, white-haired figure of the butler. His colourless eyes were fixed upon her; he spoke no word at all as, stepping aside, he gestured with a fleshless hand, indicating that the way was clear. But Laura was already stepping out into the corridor, her legs supporting her, but only just. 'I—I w-went into th-the wrong r-room . . .' He didn't believe her, of course, and she said, with a small degree of returning courage, 'Why was it left unlocked?'

'An oversight, miss.' He turned away to see to the door and Laura sped towards the wide passage leading to her room in another wing of the house.

CHAPTER FIVE

THE discovery she had made sickened her even though it did not surprise her. True, she had protested strongly when Don had mentioned the word imbecile, but his assertion that there were always foundations for gossip had left its impress and had been effective in stimulating her into making the investigation that resulted in the discovery that such an apartment did exist.

After sitting in her room for a while she glanced at the clock. It was too early to begin changing for dinner and she decided to take a stroll in the garden. Bren was there and he expressed surprise at seeing her, asking rather sharply where Francis was.

'I took it for granted you'd both gone for a walk together,' he added. He sounded rather anxious, she thought, but was reluctant to relate what she had seen.

'No, we didn't go together. I don't know where he is,' she added truthfully.

To her relief Bren did not proceed further with the matter and so she was spared the necessity of having to devise some means of shielding his cousin—for she knew she most certainly would have endeavoured to shield him. She liked Francis even though she had already discovered he was as weak as Bren was strong. She had also discovered in this short time that he was strangely subdued both by his mother and by Bren. He seemed half afraid of them, and Laura concluded that his illness had something to do with it.

'Why have you come out now?' Bren's question broke into her thoughts, startling her because she was not expecting him to be sufficiently interested in her movements. But almost immediately she guessed he was curious as to whether she was on her way to the cottage again.

'I just came out for a stroll; it's merely to pass the time until dinner's ready.' There was hardly time to visit the cottage, she could have added, but refrained.

'You obviously like walking.' Coolly sardonic his tone; Laura sensed an underlying hint of censure in this remark.

'Father and I walked great distances,' she told him, feeling shy because she had been forced to fall into step beside him in order to continue the conversation, Bren having begun to walk on again after stopping to inquire about his cousin. 'We walked every evening—when the weather was fine—both in summer and in winter.' She had ignored Bren's implication; he noticed this and there was a brief return of his arrogance in the glance he swept over her. He spoke coldly, changing the subject.

'I've had a word with my aunt about the commencement of your duties. She'll be telling you later what is expected of you.'

Laura made no comment on this. She wondered what would be his reaction were she to inform him that she had overheard his conversation with his aunt a short while ago. But of course she refrained, and they walked along in silence, Laura listening to the sough of the wind as it eerily shook the dead beech leaves still clinging tenaciously to the branches of the trees.

'I'll be going back now,' she murmured awkwardly at last, and Bren glanced down at her, his brows lifting a fraction.

'You've only just come out.' He strode along, far too quickly for her, and she was having to skip to keep up with him. 'What's the matter? Don't you care for my company?'

She looked up in surprise. Such a relaxing of his manner seemed impossible.

'I didn't expect you would want to walk with me,' she admitted frankly, and then she added, a smile trembling on her lips, 'Of course I care for your company.'

If he noted the sudden eagerness in her tones he elected to ignore it as he remarked dryly,

'I'm exceedingly flattered.' His prolonged unsmiling stare remained on her dark head. 'Tell me about your father,' he invited, surprising her yet again.

Laura continued to trot beside him, her heart light. Bren wanted her company and she no longer felt awkward. Also, all she had overheard, all her trepidation, faded into insignificance. She reflected on the way she had worshipped him from afar, content with, and grateful for, those glimpses of him each morning when she had concealed herself behind a tree or in the dense undergrowth. He had always taken the same path, and many were the times she held her breath because he stopped, glowering all around as if sensing the presence of someone other than himself. But always she had escaped detection and she would chuckle sometimes, wondering what he was thinking. Yes, she had been happy in those days to worship from a distance, never dreaming she would ever find herself walking beside him like that.

'There isn't much to tell,' she began, but went on to say her father had educated himself all his life, adding, 'You probably realized he was far superior to your other workmen?' Pride in her voice, and even a tinge of the Dewar arrogance, and fleetingly the thin, cruel mouth relaxed in a smile.

'I take it you're reminding me of his ancestry,' he commented with dry sarcasm, and before she could reply, 'I'm afraid I don't often come into contact with my workmen, especially those engaged on caring for the sheep.'

No, she knew that. Crossley was the man from whom

the men took their orders.

'Father insisted on my continuing my education after I left school,' went on Laura as they reached the end of the lake. 'He was my teacher.'

A chill breeze swept across the garden, stirring the slime on the lake; Laura drew her coat more snugly about her. Bren was in riding breeches and a long-sleeved pullover. His body seemed immune to the cold. He was hard and invulnerable, she thought, sending him a glance and noting the ruffled disorder of his wiry black hair. Yes, he was as hard as the rocks beneath their feet, the dark basaltic rocks that had defied the forces of nature for millions of years while the sediments into which they had been intruded had long since been levelled by the ruthless attacks of wind and water and ice. Aware of her prolonged interest, Bren looked down. Laura smiled at him, still palpably pleased that he desired her company even though he evinced no especial enthusiam at her presence.

He surveyed her dispassionately and said, 'Had your father any particular plans for you—seeing that he insisted on your education being continued?'

'He had ideas about sending me to secretarial school. but I wasn't enthusiastic. I don't think I'd be comfortable confined to an office stool all day.'

She laughed suddenly, her dimples very much in evidence. She was trying to draw him out, but failed. His face wore an inscrutable expression and he raised a strong brown hand to stifle a yawn. But as they proceeded he asked her more questions about her father, and her life in general. She answered in that beautifully modulated tone of hers and although she sensed that her words were not impressing him she at the same time knew instinctively that his questions were not being put merely to while away the time. He evinced curiosity regarding her life and background, and this interest sent Laura's spirits soaring to the skies. Ever since coming to the Abbey she had felt that in Bren's eyes she was considered a thing rather than a person. This interest he was now showing seemed to place her in a more favoured category; she had acquired an identity and was convinced that from now her presence would be noticed by this dark formidable man whom she loved with all her heart.

The following day she began work by sorting out Lady Margaret's wardrobe and pressing all the clothes. She had been told to do this and had half expected to find the clothes did not require pressing at all, but she was mistaken. There was not only pressing to be done, but also washing and mending. This work would keep her occupied for several days and she repeatedly thought of her promise to Don that she would be at the cottage that afternoon. She should try to get a message to him, but how? Margaret put in an appearance during the morning and Laura ventured a polite inquiry regarding her free time. The older woman was evasive, darting a glance to the garden below. Bren stood on the lawn talking to Crossley and Laura gained the impression that Margaret would have to discuss the matter of her free time with Bren before making any decision.

'I'd like to know now, if you don't mind,' persisted Laura stubbornly on receiving a second evasive answer to her inquiry.

Margaret looked slightly alarmed, a circumstance which puzzled Laura in the extreme.

'Is it important? Have you somewhere to go?'

Laura's chin lifted and two bright spots of colour touched the skin over her high, aristocratic cheekbones.

'My private life is my own, Aunt Margaret,' she said gently, 'and I prefer not to discuss it. If you will inform me when I shall be free I can make arrangements regarding the filling of my leisure time.'

Margaret's eyes glinted; she fought for control.

'Bren and I will talk the matter over later,' she began, when Laura interrupted her. She had an urgent desire to let this woman know at once that she, Laura, had a will of her own. The precise reason for this eluded her, yet she felt there was a vital necessity for showing her strength.

'It's imperative that I know before lunch, Aunt Margaret.'

Margaret's mouth compressed. She might have been born a Dewar, so ruthless and arrogant she looked.

'I'll speak to Bren at once,' and she swept haughtily from the room.

Biting her lip, Laura stared abstractedly at the pile of dresses lying on the bed. Why hadn't she practised a little more tact? She had to live with these people, was employed by them, and life could very soon become uncomfortable should strain enter into their relationships.

Bren tackled her just before lunch. She noted all the old arrogance of that first meeting with him, but as on that occasion she was not overawed by it. Nevertheless, she flushed under his severity, clasping her hands and waiting for what was to come. They had met in the hall, both being on their way to the dining-room.

'My aunt tells me you've been inquiring about your free time?' Laura merely nodded and he went on, his voice frigid and clipped, 'You were rude to her, I believe?'

'Perhaps I was a little—er—sharp,' she owned frankly. 'The reason being that Aunt Margaret seemed —well, evasive.'

'Was the matter so urgent that you required a decision immediately?'

She looked up into his face; there was a kind of warm simplicity about her which brought a strange light to his eyes. She shifted her gaze; one of his hands was tightly clenched, the knucklebones white through the tan. Suddenly she wanted to be frank with him, saying she had promised to visit the cottage again this afternoon, yet cautiously she refrained.

'It's normal for an employee to know her hours,' she said at last. She would also like to know if she were to receive wages, but that could wait for a while. The sale of her furniture and fowls had put a little money into her pocket and this she still had, practically untouched. Some of it was in Bren's safe along with her jewellery, while the portrait of William and the beautiful antiques given by him to the first Laura were in Laura's bedroom.

'We did say,' Bren reminded her, 'that you were to regard yourself as one of the family.'

She paused.

'You spoke yesterday of duties. If I have duties, then I'm an employee.'

'You sound as if you don't like the idea of being one of the family?' There was an odd inflection in his tone and his gaze was searching. It was almost as if he sensed the bewilderment and faint murmurs of apprehension that had begun to assail her.

'I can't ever be one of the family,' she told him seriously. 'On asking me to come here you gave me to understand I was to be employed as a maid-companion to Lady Margaret. I shall be content to be just that.'

His dark eyes flickered. Despite his calm control she gained the impression that he was slightly taken aback.

'Has anything happened, Laura?'

'Happened?' she echoed innocently, and his eyes narrowed in a dangerous sort of way.

'Are you being deliberately obtuse?' he inquired softly.

Her proud young head was raised; she felt half inclined to put her cards on the table and tell him all she knew, demanding at the same time a full explanation. But he was so formidable, standing there so tall and lean and arrogantly superior, his manner one of preparedness for anything she might say, that she placed a check upon her impulse and merely said she had no idea what he meant.

His mouth compressed at that and he continued to regard her through hard and narrowed eyes, but to her relief he presently gave a shrug of his shoulders and changed the subject.

'Very well, we'll let that pass for the present. Now about this free time that's troubling you. I suggest you have a couple of half days a week—Monday and Thursday, I think would suit my aunt. Are you satisfied with this arrangement?'

Monday and Thursday ... Don would in the ordinary way be working on those days and this could mean she would never see him at all. Laura looked up at Bren and said in a firm, clear voice,

'I believe it's usual, in this type of post, for an employee to have Sunday off?' It was odd that he and not his aunt should be dealing with this matter, but as this was only one of many odd occurrences she allowed it to pass without comment. However, she meant to have her Sundays off in order to continue her friendship with Don, and so that she could visit his parents with him and stay for tea as Don had suggested.

'Is there any particular reason why you should wish for Sunday off?' he asked her curiously.

'It is usual,' she repeated in the same clear tones.

The gong sounded, but neither made a move. Bren was both angry and undecided. He did not want her to see Don—for some strange reason of his own—and yet he knew she was entitled to a full day off each week, in addition to one or two half days.

'We'll discuss it some other time,' he said shortly. 'For the present you'll have the two afternoons I mentioned.'

'But...'

'Come, lunch will be getting cold.'

'Bren . . .' Laura flushed as his name fell from her lips. It was the first time she had uttered it and to her surprise he seemed to like the way she said it, for he smiled fleetingly at her before the mask of haughty indifference slipped back into place. That smile did something to her. A new and touching emotion caressed her heart like the persuasive stroke of a surgeon's hand when the beat is about to stop. Life flowed into her, exhilarating, intoxicating, and in this heady state she looked up at him, starry-eyed, her lovely lips parted as if in offering for a kiss. It was a moment of profound and unreal silence, a moment that was destined to have far-reaching effects on them both.

Bren was the first to speak; his tone was brusque to the point of harshness.

'Come,' he repeated, his long strides taking him towards the massive oak-studded door leading to the dining-room. 'The others will be waiting for us.'

Immediately lunch was over Francis made a hesitant announcement that he was going for a drive in the car, but he glanced first at Bren and then at his mother as if seeking their permission. Margaret's eyes sought those of her nephew and Laura followed their direction. Bren's face was sombrely impassive, his black eyes staring unseeingly into space. Margaret might not have been there for all the attention he afforded her. She glared at him and then, with a miraculous change of expression, she smiled at her son and suggested he take Laura out with him.

'She's worked so hard all morning,' she went on sweetly. 'So it will do her good to get out in the fresh air for an hour or two.'

'But it's Friday,' murmured Laura, her eyes drawn once more to Bren's dark impassive face. His glance flickered to hers and then away again. Francis had hesitated before agreeing to take Laura with him, but it was doubtful if this was noticed by anyone other than Laura.

'Certainly I'll take her,' he said good-humouredly, and gave her a charming and gracious smile.

'It's Friday,' repeated Laura with emphasis. She was being kept away from Don, it seemed, but she was allowed to leave her work to accompany Francis on his drive.

'Yes, dear,' said Margaret impatiently. 'I know it's Friday, but as I've just remarked, you've been hard at it all the morning and the run out will do you good. Off you go—and take care, Francis. Don't drive too fast.'

They had been on the road less than five minutes when Francis turned into a rough track and stopped the car.

'Do you really want to come with me?' he asked, and instantly Laura recalled his stealthy escape from the house yesterday afternoon. 'I mean,' added Francis when she remained reflectively silent, 'if you do, it's—it's all right, but . . .'

Laura twisted round in her seat.

'But what?' she encouraged, watching his handsome face closely.

'Well——' Impulsively he laid a hand on hers. 'Laura, I know you're a sport and can be trusted——' Again he broke off, eyeing her uncertainly in spite of his assertion that she could be trusted. 'Can I rely on you, Laura?'

'In what way?'

'Can I trust you not to say anything to my mother or Bren?'

She guessed what it was all about and told him gravely that he could trust her.

'You have a girl-friend,' she added, and his relief could be felt.

'I knew you'd be understanding. Yes, I do have a girl-friend. She's a labourer's daughter and Bren would be horrified; he's such an arrant snob. Mother might not mind so much, because she wants me to get married.'

'You'd marry this girl?'

He shrugged and frowned.

'There's no question of marriage, she knows that. Bren would put his foot down.'

Reflecting for a moment on what Mr. Dodd had said about none of the 'nobs' being interested in marrying their daughters to Francis, she wondered if he were aware of what was being said about him. Laura also reflected on what Mr. Dodd had said about Bren's having all the money and, therefore, being in a position to lay down the law.

'You can please yourself whom you marry, surely?' she commented, but Francis was shaking his head. However, he was not inclined to offer a reason for the gesture and he abruptly veered the subject.

'You don't mind about my wanting to see Meriel?'

'Is that her name? No, of course not. I suppose you want me to get out of the car?'

He glanced at her apologetically.

'Would you, Laura?'

'Certainly,' she smiled, her sympathies going out to him. His affliction was not his fault, nor was the lack of will-power and the resulting inability to assert himself. In the ordinary way Laura would have despised such weaknesses, but her father had taught her always to be tolerant of those less fortunate than herself. It was only by the grace of God, he would say, that he and she were perfect in mind and body, and she must never forget that. And so Laura had grown up with this ability to practise tolerance and understanding where it was necessary.

'You're quite sure you don't mind?' Francis was saying, and she turned.

'I don't mind in the least.' She was more than satisfied with the arrangement, but naturally kept this to herself. 'We'll go on a bit further, though,' she added, and Francis threw her a curious glance without, however, asking any questions.

'We'll have to arrive back at the Abbey together,' he said, starting up the car and backing it off the track. 'Will you meet me in about two hours' time?' He looked a trifle anxious, wondering, perhaps, what she would do with herself. Laura smiled and said,

'That will suit me admirably.'

Again she received a curious glance, but all he said was,

'You like walking, so it won't be any hardship, will it?'

'None at all.'

'Mother and Bren seem to like the idea of our being together, so perhaps you'll help me again?'

She frowned. In spite of herself she found his weakness rather revolting.

'You can get out without taking me.'

'Of course,' hastily, but he added. 'There'll be less fuss, though. It's Bren—he's always suspicious, wanting to know where I'm going and who I'm with. Anyone would think I was still a child.'

Laura made no comment; she surmised that Bren's anxiety stemmed from his cousin's illness, and that was why he wanted to know where he was going. How often did these attacks occur? she wondered. Not often, apparently, otherwise Francis would not be allowed any freedom at all. As he stopped the car on her request he once more reverted to the possibility of her helping him again.

'I'd like to see Meriel on Sundays,' he added persuasively. 'Take her out somewhere for tea. If they thought you were with me I could stay out as long as I liked. But of course you couldn't walk about all that time, could you?' He waited, sending her a sideways glance—a curious glance, as before.

'I might find a way of amusing myself.' Laura got out of the car and closed the door.

'You might?' he echoed eagerly through the open window, and Laura laughed at his expression. The conspiracy was attractive.

'I should have said I'm *sure* I'll find a way of amusing myself.'

'Laura, thanks a lot. You're a damned good sport!' In spite of his tone and the content of his words Laura did wonder if he had an inkling of her having somewhere to go. She supposed she should confide in him, the way he had confided in her, but some inner voice warned her not to do so. It behoved Francis to keep quiet about their arrangement; nevertheless, he might just make a slip some time. And Laura trembled, in spite of her innate courage, at the idea of Bren's coming to hear that she was practising deceit in order to get her Sunday afternoons off. A tiny sigh escaped her as she dwelt on this. She was her own mistress where her private life was concerned, so why this fear? Bren could do absolutely nothing should she tell him she meant to see Don on Sundays. She could demand Sundays off and threaten to leave the Abbey if he refused to agree. She had her jewellery and could sell some of it and buy a house—— But no, she would never part with Laura Vernon's treasures if she could possibly avoid it. Besides, she had no wish to leave the Abbey. Although neither comfortable nor exactly happy there, she was close to Bren whom she loved, and she could not visualize ever voluntarily cutting adrift. Unknowingly he exercised a strange compulsion on her and she sometimes wondered if it was his very ruthlessness that had captured her heart and kept it in bondage.

The sudden revving up of the engine jerked her back to her surroundings and to her companion. Francis was impatient to be off, but she stood by the car a moment to ask where Meriel lived and if she knew who he was.

'She lives in an isolated cottage with her father and an aunt. Her father works on the Duke's estate.' He nodded as he answered her second question. 'Yes, she knows who I am—but her father and her aunt don't. We meet in secret.'

Laura frowned, wondering about the girl and feeling anxious in case she should be in love with him.

The car engine throbbed again and Laura hastily fixed a time for Francis to pick her up.

'Here, then, in exactly two hours' time,' he agreed, and with a swift salute he was on his way.

The following Sunday they were off immediately after lunch. Don had informed Laura that Matthew and his wife would be at the cottage, clearing up and measuring the floors and windows for carpets and curtains. She was excited at the prospect of meeting them and although she looked rather suspiciously at Lady Margaret—on the older woman's beaming agreement that she should accompany Francis on his outing—Laura was far too pleased with the turn of events to worry her head about the odd way Lady Margaret was acting.

'We could go for a long drive and have tea out,' suggested Francis, glancing uncertainly at Bren.

'Stay out as long as you like,' his mother smiled. 'Just go off and enjoy yourselves.' She sent a flickering glance in Bren's direction. Laura had no idea what sort of response she expected, but all Margaret received was a dark glower and her own eyes glinted like steel.

How these two hated one another, she thought, sighing with relief when Francis nodded, indicating that they should be on their way.

'Laura, you look lovely!' That was the greeting she received when, after having run up the little path to the cottage, she found the door flung open before she had time to knock. The wind had tousled her hair and whipped a flush to her cheeks. She was a trifle breathless both from running and from battling against the breeze; her lips were parted invitingly and before either of them realized it she was in Don's arms and his lips were gently pressed to hers. And then he held her from him, flushing and rather boyishly embarrassed at his impulsive action. 'Must I say I'm sorry?' he began hesitantly, and Laura shook her head even as the question left his lips.

'I—I don't want you to apologize,' she murmured naïvely, allowing him to help her off with her coat. But she said no more than that, for shyness overcame her. Don immediately cleared the tension by taking her hand and showing her the sitting-room. She stood in the doorway, her appreciative glance taking in every detail of the room. Don had certainly made an excellent job of the decorating and she turned at last to extend him the praise he was eagerly awaiting.

'It's lovely. I think you're very good at your work.'

'Thanks.' He still held her hand; smilingly he asked if she were ready for a cup of tea. She nodded and within ten minutes they were sitting side by side on the box by the fire.

'When will your brother and his wife be here?' she asked him at length.

'About three. They're bringing a car-load of their things. They've no furniture to speak of, of course, having lived with Mum and Dad, but that's all ordered and should be delivered one day next week.'

'Your mother's minding the children for today?' She would have liked to meet the children, she thought, wondering whether she would take to them immediately or whether she would feel shy and awkward, never having had much to do with children.

'Yes, she's always a great help when anything's going

on—like babies arriving, and moving house,' he added with a laugh, and impulsively Laura asked him to tell her about his mother. 'She's grey-haired and a little lined—the old-fashioned sort that's becoming rare these days. She was in her thirties when she married,' he went on to explain. 'And Dad was almost forty.'

'She sounds nice.' Excitement gave a quiver to her voice. 'I'm so looking forward to meeting all your family, Don.' A wistfulness crept into her tone; he caught on to it at once and gave her hand a little squeeze.

'As I said before, you'll like every single one of them. And they'll certainly like you.'

She recalled that his mother had said things about her which weren't repeatable and a flush rose to her cheeks.

'I do hope you're right,' she said, because it was suddenly important that Don's family should like her.

'There isn't a doubt about it,' he declared emphatically, and all Laura's small fears dissolved.

'You don't mind if I carry on cleaning up this floor, do you?' he asked when they had finished their tea. Laura shook her head, offering to help. Don would not hear of it, so Laura asked if she might busy herself in the garden.

'You really want to?' But he had no need to ask. The sadness suddenly darkening her eyes told him how she had loved her garden. 'Okay then. Do just what you like out there—but mind you don't get cold. It's only February, despite the sunshine!'

'I'll come in again if I feel cold,' she promised, even while knowing she would not feel cold. She was hardy and strong in spite of her delicate appearance, for she had always worked in the garden, growing all their own vegetables when her father was alive, and keeping many hens and ducks. Several times she had tried to keep a pig, but always by the time it was half-grown she would tell her father that she couldn't possibly eat it. Whereupon he would sell it—glad to be rid of it, she felt sure, because no sooner had she said the word than it was gone.

'Pigs are a commercial proposition,' he would say. 'One is just a nuisance.'

Laura dwelt on those happy contented days as she began clearing out the old raspberry canes and tying up the new ones. There had been no complications in her life then, no fears, or prospects of loneliness, for her father was young—more like a brother to her at times. When he died at thirty-nine years of age everyone in the village was shocked, while Laura herself had for many weeks felt as if she were sinking into a black abyss where not a single glimmer of light penetrated. Even Bren was forgotten for a while. Yet it was he who unknowingly helped her to rally and to take an interest in life again, for her love for him remained strong and the diversion of seeing him each day was instrumental in bringing back the colour to her cheeks and the hope to her heart.

A car pulled up at the front gate, jerking Laura back to the present. She straightened up as the young woman got out of the car, her arms full of blankets. She stopped in the path and their eyes met. Lucy's twinkled while Laura's smiled in response—and immediately the two girls were friends.

'Hi, Laura!' hailed the elder girl unexpectedly. 'Just let me dump this lot and then I'll shake hands!'

Don came back with her; meanwhile Matt had also joined them and the introductions were made. Matt was stocky and bronzed from his work outdoors. His ready smile was a mature variety of Don's; his gaze was frank, the grip of his hand strong and sincere. Something strange welled up inside Laura, and foolishly she felt the tears pricking the backs of her eyes. These people would prove to be her true friends, she knew for sure, and this knowledge was almost too much for her emotions. However, by a tremendous effort she managed to forget the fullness within her and laughed when they teased her about the trouble she had caused them.

'I'm sorry,' she said, but Matt cut in with,

'Well, you don't look it!' and his wife then cut him short, at the same time slipping an arm round Laura's shoulders.

'You just leave her alone! How would you like to leave such an enchanting little cottage?'

Matt became grave as his eyes wandered to the open door through which could be seen the glow from the fire reflected on the newly papered walls.

'I wouldn't,' he replied softly, and turned to smile at Laura. 'Lucy and I have agreed that you must come just whenever you like,' he then told her. 'It won't be as quiet and peaceful as when you had it—not when our lively little brood are installed—but it's our sincere wish that you continue to treat it as your home.'

CHAPTER SIX

IT was five weeks since Laura first met Don's family, but already she felt she had known them all her life. On Mondays and Thursdays she would make eagerly for the cottage immediately after lunch. Lucy would allow her to busy herself in the kitchen or garden if she wished, or sometimes she would mind the baby while Lucy went into the village to do her shopping. All the children had taken to her and their delight was evident when, on those two afternoons a week, Laura would accompany their mother when she went to meet them from school. They would take the path through the woods on their way home, Lucy pushing the pram while Laura and the two little girls chased one another about among the trees. After tea Laura would tell them stories or read to them and there were always hugs and kisses for Laura when at bedtime they would insist on her helping their mother to get them ready for bed.

'Goodnight, Auntie Laura,' said Dodie one evening, and Laura felt her cup of happiness was full. It wasn't long before Lynn was also calling her Auntie Laura, and even Kevin was being taught to do so by his father. These new friendships were a source of happiness and deep contentment to Laura, but sometimes she would be troubled about the deceit she was forced to practise in order to accompany Don to his parents' house on Sunday afternoons where she would have tea, and chat for a while before returning to the Abbey in time for dinner.

After that first evasive side-tracking by Bren on her request for Sundays off Laura had again brought up the matter. There was no immediate hurry, Bren had told her curtly, and the result was that for the past five weeks she and Francis had left the Abbey each Sunday after lunch, ostensibly to drive into the country or to one of the beaches. On the way home they were supposed to stop for tea, this excuse giving them an extra hour or so. As this arrangement seemed to meet with the approval of her employer, and as it meant that Francis could meet Meriel without questions being asked, Laura decided to let it continue for a while; but she hated deceit, and she did wonder how she would keep up the deception, especially as Margaret sometimes asked about their trip—what beaches they had visited and where they had stopped for tea. Francis always came to her rescue, quite able to answer his mother's questions because he *had* been walking on a beach with Meriel, and they *had* gone to a roadside café for tea.

Another circumstance that had begun to trouble Laura was that Bren now glowered when she and Francis were preparing to leave the Abbey for their trip out. For the past two Sundays she had noticed this, and it would not have surprised her if he had firmly refused to let her go with Francis. Laura was extremely puzzled by Bren's changed attitude because on her first coming to the Abbey he had appeared more than satisfied when she and Francis walked together in the garden, or sat together on the couch, chatting. It seemed that after encouraging a friendship between her and Francis, Bren was now displeased by it. That he was displeased by her friendship with Don was even more evident, but naturally he could do nothing about it. Nevertheless, he would now and then bring the subject up and it would seem to Laura that he was probing, trying to discover just how deeply she and Don were attached. Her answers to his questions were deliberately non-committal, more owing to her reluctance to create disunity between herself and Bren than a stubborn refusal to satisfy his curiosity.

'Tell me about the others,' he requested one day after she had lightly dismissed the subject of her friendship with Don. 'They have three children, you say?'

Was he really interested? she wondered. They were having lunch—just the two of them as Margaret was out visiting her one and only relative, a great-aunt who lived over the Border, and Francis was still in bed, having had a severe attack of migraine the day before.

'Yes, two little girls—they're aged five and six—and a year-old baby, Kevin. They're cute!' she added on a note of enthusiasm, unaware of the sparkle that had entered her eyes.

'You like childen, apparently.' Bren passed her a silver basket from which she took a crispy bread roll.

'I do, yes.' She thanked him and watched him return the basket to the table. 'I hadn't had much to do with children until I made friends with Matt and Lucy, but I've discovered I love them very much. I wouldn't mind being a nanny some day,' she supplemented as the idea suddenly occurred to her.

'Nanny? Don't you want children of your own?'

A tinge of colour rose enchantingly, but she kept her eyes on Bren's face as she said,

'I'd have to be married for that, and I shall never marry.'

His eyes flickered strangely.

'You said that once before, if I remember correctly.'

Laura nodded.

'I've always known it.' Her manner was one of resignation, but she gave him a bright smile and he saw that she was in no way dejected about her intended spinsterhood. A glimmer of a smile lingered on his own lips for a few seconds and then, as on that other occasion, one of his rare laughs was heard.

'I told you you were much too young, and much too

beautiful, to be able to say a thing like that.'

Her flush deepened; he watched this rising colour with an odd expression.

'I asked you on that occasion if you had a boy-friend, and you said no.' A small pause and then, 'But you wrote each day about someone called William?' Half question, half statement. Laura's mouth curved in an amused smile. What would he do if she told him the truth? He was waiting, himself amused, for her reply and in view of what she had overheard him say to his aunt, and as Laura had no alternative than to take the easy way out, she said, avoiding Bren's gaze,

'That was just a little game I was playing.' Quite true ... but of course Bren misunderstood, believing he himself had hit on the correct explanation for the entries in that little notebook he had picked up in her cottage.

'Make-believe, eh?' She said nothing and he added, still faintly amused, 'You told me you were a romantic —because of your name, and it seems you are.'

Was he seeking a little more information as to the reason for the diary?

'Yes, because I'm descended from Laura Vernon,' was all she said, and Bren allowed the matter to drop, their lunch being eaten in silence after that. But as they both rose from the table he surprised her greatly by saying he was driving into Alnwick and she could accompany him if she wished.

'You might want to do some shopping,' he added, regarding her intently and with sudden interest because of the eager light that had entered her eyes.

'Yes, I'd love to come with you! I—I think there are one or two things I want to buy.' Laura failed to bring any to mind at the moment, but she was not unduly concerned about shopping. To be with Bren was all she desired and her heart actually thumped with excitement when, a short while later, they set out in the car for the lovely town of Alnwick.

It was a fairly long drive, through magnificent country, with the enchanting little River Coquet meandering about and the snowy summits of the Cheviots rising in the distance. The higher areas were heather-clad, with regions also of desolation where the landscape was tracts of treacherous bogs and peaty flats and dark stagnant pools, with here and there great patches of naked rock where the intrusive granite and dolerite and porphyry outcropped and lay darkly on the surface. But the steep slopes and uplands of the Cheviots provided pasture for the black-faced sheep, those hardy creatures who had retained a good deal of their wild nature and were apparently immune to the rigours of the northern winter.

Laura sat back comfortably in her seat, reflecting on the last occasion on which she had ridden beside Bren. He had brought her from the cottage to the Abbey, had been immune to her tears, impatient with her sentimentality and amused that she should crane her neck in order to take a last look at the now forlorn little building, curtainless and lost.

'It's a happy house now, though,' she murmured, flushing suddenly as Bren turned his head inquiringly.

'What did you say?'

She gave a little high-pitched laugh. 'I was thinking aloud.'

'About what?'

'The last time you drove me. I felt so unhappy...' Laura tailed off. It wasn't the thing to remind him of that little episode. However, he himself pursued the subject.

'Were you, Laura? I don't think I realized then just what you must have felt like.' A pause; Laura was faintly taken aback at the trend of conversation. 'Did I seem very heartless to you?'

How must she reply to that?

'You weren't very kind,' she said honestly at length.

Bren drove on in silence for a while.

'No, I seem to recollect a complete lack of sympathy.' He sent her a fleeting glance before returning his attention to the narrow winding road. 'Do you expect an apology—now that you know me better?'

'Oh, no!'

A smile lingered on his lips. Laura, casting him a sideways glance, recalled that he smiled more often lately—at her, that was. Not that his smiles were very much in evidence, but certainly the harsh mask would be removed on occasions.

'So you don't expect an apology,' he mused, taking a hairpin bend with expert care and skill. And he added, in the softest tones he had ever used to her, 'I'm sorry, my dear, if I seemed hard.' He became thoughtful for a space before adding, 'I didn't know you very well then—otherwise perhaps I shouldn't have been so—unkind over the affair.' His voice held regret; she told herself it was only because of his callousness on that occasion ... but for some strange reason she gained the faint impression that his regret covered something entirely different. She frowned in puzzlement, then shrugged. The impression had been transient; it left her as swiftly as it came.

Laura made no comment on his apology, for words were difficult under circumstances such as these. Bren in a soft mood was an alien to her. It seemed all wrong that he should apologize, detracting from the picture of ruthlessness and indifference to the sufferings of others. For years Laura had mentally invested him with all the vices of the Dewars. He had become the modern personification of that satanic brood, and that was the man with whom she had fallen in love. The whole village disliked the Dewars, branding them 'evil'. This widespread opinion fitted in with Laura's own picture, a picture which it would be difficult to change without some small touches of regret. And yet she recalled how, on leaving the cottage, she had desperately wanted him to notice her misery, to show some slight humanity by being sympathetic and understanding. What kind of a man would she like him to be? More important, what kind of a man was he? This softness entering into his manner with her was obviously a trait which normally lay dormant—so what other characteristics lay passive beneath that cold and harsh exterior?

His voice broke into her musings as he told her that the business he had in Alnwick would take him about an hour.

'Can you amuse yourself for that time?' he asked as they entered the tree-lined road leading into Alnwick.

'Of course. I'll look at the shops.'

'You have something to buy?'

She nodded. There were a few items she might buy, she told him.

'Might? I thought you had things you *wanted* to buy?'

'Yes...'

He turned his head. 'You're not too sure?'

Laura smiled then and owned that she had come primarily for the ride.

'It's a nice change—and I like looking in shop windows.'

'You do?' he frowned, shaking his head. 'It always seems a waste of time to me.'

'Men always think that. Father hated shopping—he always said I never knew what I wanted. But you don't, do you, until you see it?— with clothes, I mean?'

'You might not, but I do,' he returned with faint humour as he drove towards the quaint old bridge. High on the hillsides above the town stood many small mansions, and there was a blazing spread of colour from masses and masses of rhododendrons blooming in profusion in the gardens and slopes above the river, while dominating the skyline was the massive Castle of Alnwick, home of the Percy family since the beginning of the fourteenth century.

'The castle,' breathed Laura as they crossed the bridge. 'Aren't we lucky, having so many castles in Northumberland?'

'Are we?' Bren was concentrating on the traffic into which they had suddenly come on crossing the bridge.

'But of course. Everyone doesn't have such magnificent history. Did you know that William de Percy was a friend of Red de Warre? They were both with the Conqueror at Hastings.'

'I didn't know,' he commented absently, looking for a place to park. 'But I wouldn't argue about anything that occurred nine hundred years ago.'

Laura glanced uncertainly at him, but there was no evidence on his set face that he was laughing at her.

'It's quite true. This William, though, wasn't the first Percy to live at the castle. The castle wasn't there in those times—there might have been some sort of a dwelling, though,' she added for his information. 'I should imagine on a site like this, and with the river being so close, that a Saxon lord would have chosen it, wouldn't you?'

'Hmm? Oh yes, if you say so I'm sure a Saxon lord must have erected his little hut on the site.'

Her glance was decidedly suspicious now.

'Aren't you interested in history?' she queried rather stiffly.

'But of course. Aren't the Dewars—er—aren't *we* one of the most historical families in Northumberland?'

A tinkling laugh rippled; she forgot her stiff formality of a moment ago.

'I don't think you care a toss for our history!'

'I'm sure you make up for my lack of interest.' He was on the main street and had decided to turn around. 'We shall have to park outside His Grace's front door, I'm afraid.'

'Outside the castle? You're allowed to park there.'

'So I believe, but I wanted to park closer to my destination. However, the walk won't do me any harm.' Bringing the car on to a large forecourt below the towering walls of the castle, he parked it and switched off the engine.

'You know,' Laura was saying reflectively, 'it's a wonder there's any aristocracy left in England. Take the Percys, for example. The first earl to die a natural death was the fifth. The others were either killed in battle or murdered.'

'We're back to history again, are we? What do you mean, the first earl was the fifth...?' Bren had opened his briefcase and was perusing some documents he had withdrawn.

Laura heaved a sigh. 'You don't listen!'

An astounded silence filled the car. Slowly Bren brought his head round and stared at her unbelievingly. Laura bit her lip and lowered her eyes.

'Were you speaking to me?' Arrogance in his tone, soft and strongly emphasized.

'I'm sorry,' she gulped. 'I didn't mean to be rude.'

'I advise you to think before you speak in future,' he said darkly.

'Yes...' She lifted her head. 'I was telling you about the Percy's, but you didn't understand ...' Her voice trailed away into silence. Bren continued to regard her sternly for a space and then, amazingly, he softened.

'All right, tell me about the Percys if you must.'

But Laura shook her head. 'It doesn't matter. It isn't really interesting.'

'I'm sure it's exceedingly interesting. What is this about the first earl?'

She swallowed, fully aware that he was pandering to her and undecided as to whether she should answer him or insist on allowing the subject to drop. He had returned the papers to the case, which lay on his knee, and she saw that he was waiting for her to speak.

'I was saying that the first four earls died prematurely—they came to violent ends.'

'They did? Well, very few of the de Warres died in their beds, you know.'

'That's what I'm trying to point out. Always the aristocracy were being murdered or killed in wars or died in the Tower. You'd have thought half the great families would have become extinct.'

'Perhaps you've forgotten that the female could carry on the line,' he said gently.

'No, I haven't, and I know some of the husbands of heiresses took their wives' names as well as their estates, but I still think that with such a wastage of life it's a wonder our aristocracy could still flourish.' Bren said nothing, but he appeared to be interested and Laura went on, 'Going back to the Percys—the seventh earl was executed, the eighth is supposed to have shot himself in the Tower, the ninth earl was also a prisoner in the Tower for fifteen years and died because of it.'

Bren turned, his eyes opening very wide. 'You do know your history, don't you?'

'It's local history. Everyone should know what's gone on around them.'

'Tell me about the Dewars—or the de Warres, as they were then?'

Laura chuckled. 'Well, apart from slaughtering their neighbours and plundering their lands, they were often engaged in more genteel forms of killing.'

'They were? I'm relieved to hear it.'

'I'm sure you know your own history,' she retorted. 'There are dozens of books about it in your library.'

'What were these genteel forms of killing?' he wanted to know, ignoring her comment about the books.

'It was in the various wars. Two de Warre brothers,

when fighting under the red-rose banner, once boasted that they had killed fourteen Yorkists between them.'

'Nice people,' he comented, eyeing her with some amusement.

'They took part in all the wars that were going,' she went on. 'And like everyone else they were in and out of favour with the reigning monarch. Dozens of them went to the block and others died in the Tower. They were always up to some mischief or wickedness.'

'But no different from the rest at that time, I take it?'

'They were among the most bloodthirsty,' she argued. 'Rarely were they engaged in peaceful operations. Several were attainted for treason, but they were clever, apparently, because they always obtained a reversion of the attainder and their estates were restored to them.' Their titles were lost, she went on to say, when the tenure by which one of the heirs held them restricted the succession to male heirs of his alone. He died without having a son. That was Robert, as you know. Just think, if Queen Mary had not put that restriction on him you'd have had several more titles.' The present one, she knew, had been conferred on the heir, Thomas, much more recently by another monarch.

'More titles?' A sneer twisted the thin line of his mouth. 'We have more than enough!'

She had spoken without thinking and she lapsed into silence. She wondered whether the idea of finding a wife for Francis had been dropped by both Bren and Lady Margaret, or whether they were still on the lookout, as it were. Nothing was ever said about it in her hearing, and Francis obviously had no idea of what his mother and his cousing had been planning for him. He had not said he was in love with Meriel, and Laura rather thought the affair was merely a light-hearted pastime on his part. She worried sometimes about this unknown Meriel, because although Francis had told her who he was, Laura did wonder if she knew *what* he was. It seemed incomprehensible that she was in ignorance of his illness, and yet Laura herself had never heard the rumour until a couple of years ago—and even then there was nothing concrete in it. No one had ever spoken of having witnessed these periods of insanity, not even any of the various women who had worked up at the Abbey.

Bren was getting out of the car and Laura slid out from her side.

'I'll come back to the car in about an hour, shall I?' she asked, and Bren nodded.

'Don't keep me waiting,' he warned, and strode away in the direction of a small block of offices. Laura walked more slowly, stopping to window-gaze now and then, undecided about buying herself something new to wear. She did eventually buy a blouse, then strolled along the main street, casually glancing at the brass plates on the door of the low building Bren had entered. A solicitor and an estate agent, a firm calling itself Stenton's Enterprises. A fabric printers, a firm of heating engineers. Idly Laura debated on which of these interested Bren and came to the conclusion that it must be the solicitor. She frowned, sure that he would have his affairs cared for by a much larger firm than that.

The matter drifted from her mind as she strolled along. The weather was warm and sunny with clear blue skies and the pageant of spring manifested all around. The trees in the square wore the new look of bright green purity; cherry trees were laden with blossom. From the window-boxes above the shops a riot of colour tumbled down as the trailing plants left the confines of the supports provided for them.

In less than an hour Laura was back at the car, and although Bren had warned her not to keep him waiting he himself was a quarter of an hour late.

'I should have given you the key,' was all he said until they were on their way out of the town, when he added as an afterthought, 'You weren't cold?'

'No, it's a beautiful day. It's a shame to go back.' She thought of the Abbey, gaunt and grotesque, clinging like some vile parasite to the cliffs, its interior dim and eerie, its atmosphere reflecting evil deeds committed by evil occupants over long centuries of time

Bren glanced at his watch. He seemed faintly restless, she thought, as if he had something on his mind.

'We needn't go back yet.'

Her eyes opened. 'You mean ... we can go somewhere?'

There was a momentary silence as he braked behind a slow-moving car.

'Where would you like to go?'

Laura was so stunned she said the first thing that entered her head.

'Anywhere—I don't mind at all so long—so long ...' Her words rolled off into silence. Laura searched for something to add to her unfinished sentence.

'So long as what?'

'So long as you are there.' What would he say if she gave the intended completion to her words? It was fortunate indeed that she had pulled herself up in time.

'So long as it's nice and pleasant,' she finished lamely, and a strange silence ensued before he spoke.

'I can't think of anywhere—around here—that isn't nice and pleasant.' He was driving fast, having overtaken the dilatory man who had been holding him up. 'How about Warkworth Castle for a start?'

She blinked. 'Warkworth Castle?' For a start, he had said. It would take an hour and a half to go over Warkworth Castle.

'You can get talking to the custodian and gen yourself up on the Percys,' he returned with a laugh.

Laura just could not believe it. Never had she seen Bren in a mood like this. He was a totally different being from the coldly arrogant man to whom she was used.

However, she immediately fell in with his suggestion, receiving what was offered without question. It was abundantly clear that there was more to Bren's character than that veneer of austerity, and Laura was curious to learn something about it.

'You've been before?' inquired Bren after a while.

'Not inside. Father never had money for such things.'

Bren twisted his head to look at her with a faintly admonishing light in his eyes.

'I still can't understand why you hoarded all that wealth.'

'It was Laura Vernon's,' she returned simply.

'I rather think Laura wouldn't have minded in the least if you'd bought yourselves a little comfort with her treasures.'

'Perhaps not,' agreed Laura, settling back comfortably for the seven-mile drive. 'But it would have troubled our consciences had we let her things go to strangers.'

'Are you going to keep them for ever?'

'Of course.' She looked out towards the distant rising massif of the Cheviots. The wild windswept uplands would be ablaze with gorse now, golden in the sunshine, spraying the air with its deliciously fragrant perfume.

'I've always said I'd climb the Cheviot one day,' she commented, speaking her thoughts aloud. 'I can do it in an afternoon.'

'You'll have to wait a while; mists still come down fairly often.'

'Yes—I'll do it next month, probably.'

Soon they were entering the village of Warkworth, nestling in the horseshoe bend of the River Coquet. The castle was on a hill and they climbed steeply towards it, coming round so as to approach it from the south, from where the view of it was breathtaking, for it could be seen as a whole. Here only was there a moat, as on all other sides the promontory fell steeply away so that no added protection was considered to be necessary.

They parked the car and paid their money. The man in the office offered to go round with them, but Laura looked up at Bren and said hesitantly,

'We could manage with a guide-book.'

His brows lifted and a hint of amusement was revealed in the crinkly lines appearing at the corners of his eyes.

'Do you really require one?' he asked, putting his hand in his pocket and producing the money.

'It's not for the history, but the plan.'

They went in without a guide and after wandering through the Chapel and Great Hall, exploring the three floors of the keep, and ascending stairs to various towers they sat down on a grassy bank above the tree-lined river.

'Isn't it peaceful?' she murmured. Her eyes were bright but wistful. She began to doubt whether it had been a good idea, coming out like this with Bren. It was rather like tasting the nectar of the gods and knowing it was the one and only time she would do so. For it must be quite beyond the bounds of possibility that she would ever find herself in a position like this again.

'Come,' he said, with a return of that restlessness she had previously noticed. 'We'll drive for a while.' Rising, he watched her put the guide book in her handbag. She glanced up at him and a half smile quivered on her lips. Her hair had fallen forward and she brushed it from the side of her face; he saw the flush on the lovely cheeks, the wistful shadow in her soft brown eyes. Stirring abruptly, he reached down with an involuntary movement and Laura put her hand in his, surprise quenched by the exquisite pain of finding her small hand clasped strongly in his. She came up close to him, the rough tweed of his coat brushing against her cheek. They stood for one moment of eternity, hands clasped, eyes meeting. Something stirred in Laura's heart; she wondered if he could hear its loud irregular throbbing. His jaw tightened as if at some secret thought, and Satan himself looked out of those lawless eyes. He might have had murder in his heart, she thought, for the lust for blood seemed to be reflected in his gaze. She shuddered, yet was unafraid. He relaxed and the softness returned to the thin cruel mouth. He smiled faintly down at her, his gaze shifting to the tiny hand he held in his. Turning his own hand over, he allowed hers to lie on his palm and his long brown fingers passed half caressingly over the smooth white skin. Slowly he closed his hand until hers was lost. 'We'll drive into the hills,' he declared abruptly, retaining his hold as they walked to the car.

They traversed wild country, the most beautiful and varied in the whole of the British Isles. It was as if they had the world to themselves, up there in the hill regions of the Cheviots. They had got out of the car and walked, in silence most of the time, for Bren was lost in thought. And wild he looked, his face to the wind, his eyes narrowed against the sun. The wiry black hair fell on to his low-lined brow, the line of his profile might have been cut in stone by some classical sculptor of a pagan age. He strode along as if he had not a moment to spare, oblivious of the trotting girl beside him. Desolate the scene became, with wild and picturesque chasms splitting the rocks, and great crags rising steeply on either side of them. From the snowy summit of the Cheviot, the highest point in the Cheviot Range, a frothing burn issued from a terrifying gorge to splash its way from ledge to ledge for nearly one thousand five hundred feet, wearing mercilessly away at the resistant rocks which must in the end succumb and end up as sediment in the sea. With the hope of slowing her companion down Laura remarked on the series of waterfalls made by the burn on its downward race from the top of the Cheviot.

'They're pretty, don't you think?' she added breathlessly. 'Shining like that in the sun?'

'Pretty but transient. All waterfalls are doomed—even Niagara.' It was a statement; she knew it was a fact but felt that he had merely spoken automatically.

'Only transient in geological time,' she reminded him. 'It will take millions of years for the water to wear away those hard bands of rock.'

Bren turned to look down at her. 'You know your geology as well as your history,' he remarked, still striding along at a tremendous pace.

'Father taught me these things about the land. I like to know why there should be a mountain here or a cliff there or a valley down below. I like to look at the landscape around me and know just how it came to take a particular form.'

'Most people would just enjoy the scenery and not trouble their heads as to how it was formed.'

'Yes, I expect so.' Too breathless to talk any more, she just continued to trot along beside him, wondering if eventually he would become tired. She looked down at the river, now far below, winding about and flowing swiftly, fed by the countless burns tumbling down from the Cheviot Hills.

'Are you tired?' Bren inquired unexpectedly.

'I am rather breathless,' she returned with a quick, apologetic laugh. 'If you could slow down a little it would be more comfortable.'

'Going too fast for you, am I?' He slowed his pace and Laura breathed a sigh of relief. 'You're enjoying it, though?' He glanced at her again, but disinterestedly. His mind was still on other things.

'Yes, I'm enjoying it.'

'You like the wild country?'

She nodded. A ruined peel tower cut into the sky some great distance away. How lonely it was! Laura fell into a reverie as she pictured the occupants, long ago, housing their cattle in the lower rooms of their fortified dwelling, hiding them from the moss troopers and reivers who, between autumn and spring, lived the rough existence of riding the foray, pillaging the land as they did so and stealing their neighbours' sheep and other livestock.

What a wild and bloodthirsty history Northumberland had! Laura envied those people living in the stirring times of the Border raids. She would have enjoyed living dangerously, she thought.

Her meditations were interrupted by Bren's voice, low and sharp.

'We'd better turn back. There's a mist coming up.'

They were almost in the peat-bog country, where black stagnant pools contributed to the formation of mist. Bren wheeled about; Laura did likewise and they began to retrace their steps. But within minutes they were in a damp and vaporous world of silence. Laura shivered and to her astonishment Bren put an arm about her shoulders, drawing her to him. She felt his warmth through his coat. She smiled a thank-you, feeling small beside him, but so very safe.

Their way being downhill they were not long in leaving the mist behind and emerging into the sunlight again. But the sun was dropping now and the profile of the hills was black against a sky of copper and gold.

'We've been out a long while,' commented Laura conversationally as Bren released her, obviously assuming that she no longer felt the cold.

'We'll stop somewhere on the way back and have a meal.'

'Stop?' Laura twisted her head to stare at him. What was the matter with him today? Had something gone wrong?—something which made him reluctant to return to the Abbey? He certainly appeared to have no desire to do so. 'You mean have dinner out?'

He nodded, striding along now, indifferent to the fact that she was being forced to trot again.

'We'll dine at an inn I know. They usually make a very good meal.' He smiled at her and added, 'We're both ready for something to eat, I'm thinking.'

'Well, I must admit I'm hungry, but what about Aunt Margaret? She'll be expecting us to be back for dinner.'

'Then she'll be disappointed,' he returned crisply, and Laura let the matter drop.

They had almost reached the car, but the sun had still not disappeared altogether, and Laura gave a little gasp of appreciation and wonderment.

'It's so beautiful down here—and yet up there you could almost believe you were in a different country.'

'It was rather bleak, once the mist rose,' he agreed. And then, 'You were talking about climbing to the top. I think you'd better not go alone.'

'I'll be all right,' she returned carelessly. 'I'm not going until the beginning of the summer.'

'Even then you'd better not go alone.' The voice was stern all at once, and inflexible. Was he giving her an order? Laura's proud little chin rose and a sparkle entered her eyes.

'I'm quite capable of taking care of myself,' she told him in firm decisive tones.

Bren almost stopped. 'What do you mean by that statement?' he demanded, an even more severe edge to his voice.

'I meant that I'll go when—when I feel like it——' But she broke off, because now he *had* stopped and he was staring down at her with that look of frigid hauteur which had characterized his manner towards her on their very first meeting.

'You will?' he said gently, his eyes narrowing. And when she prudently refrained from answering, 'I think not, Laura. It's not safe for you to go up there alone and I forbid you to do so. Understand?'

She bit her lip. Bren made no effort to walk on again and she had to stand there, her hands clasped in front of her, her head lowered.

'I—you——' She looked up. 'I'm not used to taking orders,' she told him. 'If you *asked* me not to go——'

'So you're not used to taking orders, eh? Well, you'll take one now. You're not to go up there alone. That's my final word and if you should be contemplating disobeying it I advise you to think again.' And with that he walked on and soon they were parking the car in the forecourt of an hotel in Bamburgh.

It was natural that a little constraint should follow his brusquely spoken order and silence reigned for a while after they had sat down. But the warmth of the atmosphere and effect of the wine were soon instrumental in thawing both Laura and her companion and during the meal they chatted freely—while never once mentioning the Abbey or its two other occupants. It was as if by common consent the subject was taboo.

An hour and a half later they emerged into a purple velvet night where a half moon shone gently through the glittering brilliance of a star-studded sky.

'This is wonderful!' Laura threw back her head and breathed deeply. What a wonderful afternoon and evening it had been, she thought as she took her seat in the car and closed the door. Pity one had to go home after such bliss——

'We'll have a turn on the shore.' Abruptly Bren's voice cut into her thoughts and again she started in surprise. Was he as unenthusiastic as she about returning to that dark and dismal house? Surely not. It was his ancestral home where for centuries his family had lived.

'I love the shore at night,' she was saying a short while later as they strolled together along the sands at Seahouses. Bren was in no hurry this time, his restless mood having disappeared. 'It's so different from the daytime—so profound and unreal.'

He glanced down at her but said nothing; they walked on in companionable silence, and for a long while there were no other sounds but the primeval ones of wind and surf. Clouds masked the moon and a sudden blackness fell, enshrouding the water and the beach. Instinctively Laura moved closer to Bren; he felt her body by his side and for the second time that day he slipped his arm about her shoulders.

She closed her eyes. The world did not exist in this vast impenetrable void in which she and Bren were poised. Fenstone Abbey was a million light years away. In the unearthly darkness Bren stopped, drawing her close as one hand slid to her waist. The tips of his long slender fingers tilted her chin and his head came down, his lips lightly caressing her forehead and her cheek on their way to her mouth. She trembled against him and was drawn closer still; her trembling increased as a spasm of ecstasy shot through her.

So this was the real awakening ...

No words passed between them as a little while later they walked on again. The half-disc emerged from behind the scudding clouds and there was light again and the world appeared once more.

Silhouetted against the sky was the Castle of Bamburgh, crowning the impressive headland which was a disconnected part of the quartz dolerite forming the Great Whin Sill, that intrusive mass which, having in some far-off age of upheaval forced its way into the sedimentary rocks, today affected Northumberland's scenery in the most attractive way. It had provided some of its coasts with intricate outlines, and produced the fine headlands at Dunstanburgh and at Cullernose Point, in addition to that at Bamburgh. The igneous mass reappeared in the Farne Islands, outliers of the Whin Sill, now disconnected by the forces of erosion. Inland the dolerite sill formed picturesque crags and was often followed by Hadrian's Wall; in other places it gave rise to steep-faced escarpments, or to waterfalls where its hard rocks endured after the softer shales and sandstones had been worn away.

'I suppose,' said Bren as a strong offshore breeze blew up to oppose the rolling waves, 'that we should be thinking of going home.'

She nodded in the darkness. The prospect was far from attractive. There was Lady Margaret, for one thing. Laura had a strong suspicion that she would be far from pleased at their excursion. And as she thought of this there came to Laura's mind that sentence she had heard uttered by her employer after she had seen Laura and Bren walking together in the garden. 'We don't want her falling in love with *you*!'

No, Lady Margaret would be far from pleased that Laura and Bren had spent the whole afternoon and evening together.

Sitting beside Bren in the car on the way home Laura once again brought that sentence to mind. The emphasis on the last word was obviously significant, and at the time Laura had naturally puzzled over it before impatiently putting it out of her mind. It was part of the mystery, she had told herself—but now there did not appear to be a mystery after all, for during the past five weeks her life had run smoothly and she had almost forgotten her earlier misgivings as to the Dewars having some ulterior motive for bringing her to their home. She worked—spasmodically, it was true—for Lady Margaret, looking after her clothes and keeping her bedroom in order—for Margaret was anything but tidy in her ways. On occasions there would be dusting and cleaning downstairs, because the one and only maid was a 'daily' and if one of her family happened to be off colour then she would fail to put in an appearance.

Laura's reflections ceased as the Abbey came into view. Perched on its crags, its fortified turrets cutting into the purple sky, it looked like some giant prehistoric monster clawed motionless to the rocks. She swallowed, and turned her head to glance at Bren. His lean angular face was taut, his lips compressed. She could not see his eyes in the dimness, but somehow she knew they were staring with hatred at the decaying pile that was his home.

CHAPTER SEVEN

LADY MARGARET'S reaction to the little outing was never made known to Laura, and the only visible sign of displeasure was an occasional baleful glance in her nephew's direction. Laura was treated with the usual smiling civility by her employer and Laura felt totally indifferent to anything unpleasant which might have transpired between Lady Margaret and her nephew. They had told her to consider the Abbey as her home. It could never remotely resemble home and now that she had friends Laura considered the Abbey merely as a place of employment, her leisure time being spent entirely with Don and his family.

Sometimes Don would question her about her life up at the big house. She disliked talking about it, but on occasions she would oblige, aware that he was still anxious about her, still uncertain about the uncharacteristic behaviour of the Dewars in offering Laura a home. His eyes would become dark and brooding as she talked and at times it seemed to Laura that they held a secret which he was on the point of revealing, but refrained.

On the Sunday following her trip out with Bren Laura was standing in the hall waiting for Francis to come downstairs when Bren emerged from the room at the end, which was his study. His glance moved from Laura to Francis and his dark eyes seemed suddenly to smoulder.

'You're going out?' He spoke to Francis, who had reached the bottom stair. 'Not with Laura?' Clipped and curt the question. Laura looked at Bren uncomprehendingly. Neither he nor she had ever referred to that moment on the sands when he had taken her in his arms and kissed her. In ordinary circumstances that kiss would have been unaccountable, but Laura now regarded it as a part of his strange mood of that particular day. His silence and his brooding distance, his wild excursion into the desolate heights of the Cheviots, his reluctance to return to his home—all these added up to some form of overstrained emotions into which that kiss fitted like the final piece of a jigsaw puzzle. It had been passionless, even though it had awakened her. It had not the sweetness or the intimacy of that moment in the garden, that moment when she had let his name fall involuntarily from her lips for the first time and had drawn a smile from him in response. They had been linked for a few moments in some unforgettable way.

'But of course with Laura. We always go out on Sunday afternoons.'

A small silence and then, peremptorily,

'You're not taking her today. You're not—er—well.'

Laura blinked. Why the hesitation? And was Francis unwell?

'Are you insinuating that I'm not capable of driving the car?' he asked unsteadily.

'I'm not insinuating, I'm stating.'

Laura felt troubled. She was going to Don's parents' house for tea. They were expecting her and would have it ready. Don would be waiting for her by the bridge in the village.

'Laura and I are going out,' declared Francis, but his tones were nervously slurred and indistinct.

'I think not.' Soft words, but inflexibly pronounced. Laura knew for sure that she would not be going out with Francis that afternoon. She watched him, waiting for his reaction, aware as she was of the weakness of his character. His handsome face became blotchy, his eyes stared from their sockets. He *was* ill, she thought, glancing at Bren. Sneering contempt was portrayed both in the twist of his mouth and the sweep of his eyes as they moved slowly over the whole length of his cousin's body. How callous—to evince not the slightest degree of pity for a man who was obviously feeling off-colour. What was wrong with Francis? He seemed rather unsteady on his feet.

'Then—then I'm going out on my own!' There was an effort at defiance in his tone which was apparently unnecessary as far as Bren was concerned, because he said,

'Please yourself about that——' But he was interrupted by the appearance of his aunt from the sitting-room. She looked questioningly from Bren to Francis and then asked what it was all about.

'He says Laura can't come out with me,' her son replied, glaring at Bren.

Arrogant eyes turned upon Bren. 'Perhaps you'll explain?' she invited frigidly.

The twist of his lips transformed itself into a thin straight line.

'Do I ever explain my actions? Laura stays in because it's my wish that she stays in!'

Margaret's dark eyes smouldered; they moved slowly from Bren to Laura, an odd expression in their depths.

'Francis and Laura always go out together on Sunday afternoons.' She looked squarely at her nephew. 'Why the sudden objection, may I ask?'

'I've just said Laura stays in; that's sufficient!'

Laura felt her temper rise. But then it suddenly occurred to her that Sunday was not her day off and so Bren was within his rights to refuse to let her go out with Francis. Had this scene occurred on one of her free half-days she would not have stood here so meekly and been told what she must or must not do!

'I'm going on my own,' repeated Francis with a spurt of bravado which was yet accompanied by a rather uncertain glance in his mother's direction.

'On your own? Where would you go on your own?' she wanted to know, frowning at him.

'I'll drive around.'

'Good idea. Then if he kills someone it will only be himself.'

'Bren!' His aunt glared at him evilly. The age lines on her dark face deepened; a lock of metallic black hair fell on to her forehead. She looked a she-devil, thought Laura, her thoughts partly on Don, who would be waiting there, by the bridge, becoming more and more anxious with every moment that passed. She became aware of Margaret's eyes fixed upon Bren as the woman said slowly, and somehow significantly, 'I do believe you wouldn't care if he did kill himself,' but the words were muttered, for the woman seemed to be merely voicing her thoughts and not talking to her nephew at all.

'Don't be melodramatic,' drawled Bren, bored now, to all outward appearances. 'Laura, you can go and take off your coat.'

She bit her lip, thinking again of Don. She had a shrewd suspicion that he would not hesitate to come up to the Abbey if she failed to put in an appearance at the appointed time.

'May I go for—for a walk?' she asked, meeting Bren's gaze with difficulty. 'I feel like a breath of fresh air.'

He examined her face. 'You're pale,' he observed. 'Are you unwell?'

A little sagging of relief took place inside her. All unknowingly he was assisting her.

'Not exactly, but I would feel better for a walk.' Which was perfectly true even though she *had* twisted the truth slightly.

'Yes, off you go, then——'

'Just a moment, Bren,' his aunt interrupted haughtily. 'I believe it's I who should give Laura leave to go out. I could be desiring her services this afternoon!'

An expression of arrogance returned to Bren's eyes; they swept his aunt from head to foot.

'You *weren't* requiring her services,' he reminded her softly. And then, to Laura, 'Go for your walk, child, and get the colour back into those cheeks.'

She smiled her thanks and without so much as a glance in his aunt's direction swiftly made her escape.

She had to run all the way, but she was still late on arrival at the bridge where Don was waiting.

'I'm so sorry,' she said breathlessly. 'I was delayed.' Don was in ignorance of the arrangement she had with Francis. He had concluded that her Sundays were free and Laura had seen no necessity for disillusioning him. Now, however, she was to experience some difficulty in explaining that she could not stay out too long. 'I'll have to be back at the Abbey for tea,' she began, when he interrupted her, surprise on his handsome boyish face.

'Back at the Abbey? But for the past five weeks you've had tea with Mum and Dad. They're expecting you.'

'I'm terribly sorry,' she faltered. 'But—but——' There seemed nothing for it but to tell him the truth, which she did, reluctantly, because it seemed to throw a bad light on Bren. Don was silent for a long while after she had finished speaking and as she turned to cast him a sideways glance she recalled her impression that he had some secret knowledge he would like to impart to her but which he deliberately held back for some reason of his own.

'So it would have been all right for you to stay out, had you been with Francis?—had they *thought* you were with Francis, that is?'

She nodded, but frowned at the same time.

'It was Lady Margaret who wanted me to be with Francis,' she reminded him.

Another silence. They were almost at the top of the

hill leading out of the village. This was the way they always took because just over the hill was the main road and the bus stop where they boarded the bus which would take them to the pretty little seaside village where Don's parents lived.

'Laura——' Don stopped on the path and turned to face her. 'Will you answer me a question?'

'Of course?' she smiled.

'Bren, do you . . . trust him, implicitly?'

Her brown eyes opened very wide; Don's own eyes flickered perceptively and a deep shuddering sigh escaped him.

'But most certainly!' came the half angry, half indignant retort. 'I'd trust Bren with my life!'

'Don't misunderstand me,' he said after a pause. 'I'm not suggesting he would do you any personal harm——'

'Indeed I hope you're not!' She was recalling that long and lonely tramp when she and Bren had shared a vast solitude up there in the hills. Fear had never touched her for one fleeting second. She could travel into eternity alone with Bren and be safe.

For a long moment there was silence between them, then Don gave a shrug of resignation and they began to walk on again.

'What shall we do, then?' he asked at last. 'You can stay out no more than a couple of hours, you say?'

'That's right. I must be back for tea.' She paused; for the first time there was constraint between them and Laura felt unhappy because of it. 'I'm sorry if I was sharp,' she said, turning to him as they walked along. 'But I can't let anyone say things about Bren in my hearing.'

'I understand, Laura.' He spoke a trifle stiffly, but it was the cryptic note in his voice that arrested her. What did he understand? Should she ask him? But no, she was not entering into any conversation where anything derogatory could be said about Bren. Working on the estate, Matt had probably heard gossip about the Dewars—unsavoury gossip, that was for sure—and if this gossip had been passed on to Don then that accounted for his anxiety. But she had nothing to fear. As she had so emphatically declared, she would trust Bren with her life.

They decided to spend the remaining hour or so on a visit to the cottage, for there was no time to go to Don's home. Matt was in the garden and his eyes opened with surprise on seeing them come through the gate.

'Anything wrong?' he asked, looking a trifle anxiously from one to the other.

'Not really.' Don closed the gate after Laura, and waved a hand to Lucy, who was at the kitchen window. 'Laura's to be back at the Abbey in about an hour's time, so we've come here instead of going home.'

Lucy had come out to see what was wrong and Don repeated the explanation. Laura felt utterly miserable, not only at disappointing both Don and his parents, but at the loss of her own pleasure, for she thoroughly enjoyed her visits to the Saunders' pretty cottage.

'Why have you to be back?' Lucy wanted to know. 'Is her ladyship ill, or something?'

Laura shook her head; Don looked at her and asked if he could tell them the reason for Laura's being unable to stay out.

'Yes, you might as well.'

They all went into the house, and Laura immediately moved over to the pram where Kevin lay, peacefully enjoying his afternoon nap, the two girls being at Sunday School. Kevin lay on his side, sucking his thumb. A wistful expression entered Laura's eyes. If she hadn't fallen in love with Bren she might some day have married and had a baby like this. But she had fallen in love with Bren, had been in love with him ever since she could remember—or so it seemed, for she could not recall a time when she had not been acutely aware of him, living up there in the house on the crags, and taking his walk through the woods every morning and always at the same time. He would brave most weathers, she recalled, and only when the rain poured down or the snow fell heavily did he fail to take his walk. Kevin stirred but did not wake, and Laura left him to take a seat by Don on the couch. Matt was gazing at her rather oddly when she glanced up, but both he and Lucy were tactfully silent about the information just imparted to them by Don. Lucy busied herself making tea and this was brought in, along with freshly baked cakes and biscuits.

'Come on,' urged Matt. 'You're not eating anything.'

Laura smiled and took a cake from the plate offered.

'Thank you, Matt.' She cast Don a sideways glance; he turned and she whispered, her lip trembling, 'I'm so sorry, Don.' He smiled then; the strain between them was removed and the conversation began to flow in its normal way.

'Shall we tell her?' queried Lucy after a while, and Matt grimaced.

'Dare we?'

Laura looked blankly from one to the other. 'What is it?'

'We're going to knock the cottage about something shocking. We've asked Mr. Dewar to have another bedroom built on, and so Matt's having a garage as well.'

'Oh . . .' The character would be gone, Laura felt sure. But she managed to smile as she said, 'That should be much more convenient for you.'

'We do need the extra bedroom,' put in Matt. 'We've only the two, as you know, and that means Kevin is in with us. He should be in a room on his own.'

'They're going to use the local stone,' Lucy informed her swiftly. 'So it shouldn't look like a modern addition. We wouldn't like that ourselves; we want it to blend in.'

'When did you get Bren's agreement to this?' Laura inquired on a curious note.

'Matt asked him as soon as we moved in, but he wouldn't give us an answer right away. They don't, do they, not those sort of people. They have to think about it for a while. However, he hasn't kept us waiting too long. He told Matt on Friday that he'd arranged for an architect to come and take a look, and draw up the plans.'

He hadn't said anything to her, mused Laura. But of course he would not consider it was any of her business what he did with his property. Laura looked around. Her new friends had it tastefully decorated and furnished, and she was sure she did not envy them the cottage . . . but nostalgia still assailed her at times, especially if she happened to be on her own for a few moments when Lucy was upstairs or outside in the garden, pegging washing on the line. Laura's thoughts would then wander to the past and she would remember the contentment of being with her father and the tears would come very close to being shed. Bren had not understood because he had no idea what it was like to feel sentimental about one's home. He could never imagine the wrench of leaving or the agony of wondering what sort of people were going to take one's place. But since then he had admitted to a lack of sympathy—had even gone as far as to make an apology! Yes, he had a softer side to him, she had now discovered, and wondered if, had he his time over again, he would allow her to remain in the cottage. If he had done so then these charming people would still be without a home, and she would never have met them. One could not have everything, and she was so glad she had these friends.

'I'd better go and pick up those two rascals,' Matt

was saying a short while later. 'I'll not be long. You won't be gone before I come back?' He looked at Laura, who glanced at the clock and shook her head. 'I'll run you home, then,' he offered, and went out to start the car.

Less than fifteen minutes later the two little girls came bounding into the room.

'Auntie Laura! I didn't think you'd be coming to see us today! We wouldn't have gone to Sunday School if we'd known!' Lynn flung her arms round Laura's neck and gave her a loud kiss on the mouth.

'How long are you staying?' Dodie came more slowly, but gave Laura a hug and a kiss. 'Are you and Uncle Don having tea with us?'

'Not today, Dodie,' Laura smiled, making room so that the two children could sit down on the couch. 'Tomorrow I'll be coming for tea.'

'Not today?' wheedled Lynn.

'Auntie Laura can't, dear,' put in Lucy. 'You'll just have to be patient and wait until tomorrow.'

The time passed all too swiftly and Laura sighed deeply when at four o'clock she rose from the couch and said she must be going.

'Make my apologies to your mum and dad, won't you?' she said on getting out of the car. Don had ridden with her and Matt was taking him home after dropping Laura. 'Tell them I'm terribly disappointed at not being able to come.'

'Shall I tell them you'll come next Sunday?' They were parked a few yards from the gate, completely sheltered from view by the massive yew hedge running along that side of the garden. 'Will you be able to get out, do you think?'

'I should be able to. Francis won't make the same mistake again.' Automatically she put a few paces between her and the car, and Don followed her.

He shook his head. 'It isn't a very satisfactory arrangement, Laura,' he said on a wrathful note. 'Your Sundays should be your own. You're not a slave.'

'Slave?' She managed a little laugh. 'I scarcely do any work at all.'

'Perhaps I should have said—you're not a prisoner . . . or are you?'

A flush spread; she glanced at Matt, sitting in the car, waiting for his brother. He could not hear, she realized, and resumed her conversation with Don.

'I'll insist on having my Sundays off,' she decided, a sparkle in her eye. 'Yes, Don, you can tell your parents I'll be there next Sunday.'

'All right, I will.' He hesitated a moment and then, seriously, 'There are things I can't talk about, Laura—not in view of what I now know——'

'What you now know?' she interrupted, puzzled. 'I don't understand?'

'I realize you don't, but I can't explain, so please let the matter drop.' He spoke persuasively yet firmly and she did not pursue the matter. 'What I can say is this,' he then went on, 'if you should ever think of leaving the Abbey I want you to know you have friends.' He looked straight at her. 'You have me, but you also have Matt and Lucy and my parents—we all care about you, Laura. Please remember that and if ever you find yourself in difficulty then you must come to us—promise?'

'I shan't have to leave the Abbey,' she began, when he interrupted her.

'You can't say a thing like that. None of us can foresee the future. Have I your promise that you will come to us if ever you need help of any sort?'

She nodded, but gave a small sigh at the same time. From the first Don had not liked her being up at the Abbey, and had even tried on one or two occasions to persuade her to find a job elsewhere. He never said so, but Laura gained the impression that he thought she might come to some harm, but she knew that was quite impossible, because Bren was there.

'Yes, I promise.' And Laura did not say any more than that because she had been out much longer than the two hours she had allowed herself.

On her arrival at the Abbey she found Bren alone in the sitting-room, and when she tentatively inquired about Francis she was told he had gone out on his own.

'I'll go and get on with my work,' she began when Bren told her to sit down, indicating a chair facing him. She obeyed, feeling a little apprehensive under his searching scrutiny.

'Aunt Margaret is lying down, with a headache,' he told her, 'so you can't busy yourself in her room.' Again he scrutinized her for a long moment before he said, very softly, 'Where have you been?'

Her chin lifted. 'For a walk.'

Bren's eyes opened very wide. 'Be careful, Laura. I asked you where you had been.'

'Surely that's my own affair?'

'I gave you time off to take a walk,' he reminded her. 'I'd like to know how far you walked.'

Laura tilted her proud head and looked him squarely in the eye. There was no reason at all why she shouldn't admit to having been to the cottage—she could easily do this without mentioning her assignation with Don—but she stubbornly refused to satisfy Bren's curiosity. Much as she loved him she could not excuse conduct such as this. Her life was her own and he must be made to accept the fact.

'You did give me time off, yes,' she agreed in a faintly quivering voice. 'And I want to speak to you about my Sundays. I want to have them off—the afternoons, at least.' She had ignored his question and although his gaze darkened and his jaw went taut he let the matter rest as he dealt with her request.

'For the past five weeks you've had your Sunday afternoons,' he reminded her. 'You've been out with Francis.'

'It could be,' she commented, avoiding his gaze, 'that I might just want to go off on my own. What then?'

'You're not happy with Francis?' he queried sharply, and Laura frowned. Why did he regard her in this curious way? Why was he waiting so tensely for her reply?

'I enjoy his company, yes, but I have friends, and I would prefer to visit them on Sundays.'

'You'd *prefer* to visit them?' Soft tones, edged with the most odd inflection. 'You'd rather be with these friends than with Francis?'

She nodded.

'I like Don's parents——' The words were out before she realized they could be damning. She moistened her lips, waiting for the silence to end. But it continued for some seconds before Bren said, again in that softly modulated tone,

'I understood you to say you spent your free time at the cottage. You told me you went there on Mondays and Thursdays and stayed for the whole of the afternoon and evening.'

'Yes, I d-do—but I've met Don's parents and—and they've asked me to-to tea. I could go there on Sundays.' How difficult it was to embark on deceit with him regarding her in that searching way.

'I see,' he murmured after a long moment of thought. 'So if you were free on Sundays you'd be with Don and his parents?'

She nodded, wishing she could dislodge the tightness in her throat. How much longer was this questioning to continue?

'Yes, I'd be with them every Sunday.' Bren was staring into the fire and after a moment she added, 'Can I have Sundays off, then?'

A frown crossed the dark brow. 'This Don,' he said, 'how important is he to you?'

Laura flushed. 'He's one of my friends.'

'A special one, though, I assume?'

He had asked her about 'William', she recalled, and now he was curious about Don.

'Not in the way you're suggesting,' she truthfully replied.

'The way I'm suggesting?'

'It sounded as if you were inquiring about the seriousness of our friendship.'

A short pause and then,

'Perhaps I was. How serious is it?'

'We're only friends—I've just said he isn't a special friend.'

Bren looked at her.

'He could be, perhaps?' on a curious note.

Laura shook her head, reminding him that she had said she would never marry. And before he had time to comment she added insistently, 'Can I have my Sundays off?'

He gazed into the fire, his face harsh and his jaw flexed. He seemed reluctant to answer her. She sensed the fury within him and was amazed by it.

'I've already discussed this with my aunt,' he said at last, the words issuing from between tight lips, 'and she says she needs you on Sundays.'

'Needs me?' Laura stared in disbelief. What a weak statement!—and coming from Bren. His word was law, she knew that, and if he had decided she have Sundays off then Margaret would have had to abide by it. 'She *needs* me?' Laura looked suspiciously at him, but he was still staring into the fire and she was unable to read his expression. 'How can she say that, when I'm out with Francis every Sunday afternoon?' Her cheeks were flushed with anger. There was something distinctly odd about this apparent flaw in Bren's strength. 'Can it be that *you* don't want me to have the time off?'

'You happen to be employed by my aunt,' he reminded her, a fleck of ice entering his voice. 'It is for her to decide what days you shall have off.'

Laura bit her lip. What must she do? Don had received her promise that she would visit his parents next Sunday, but as she looked at Bren's hard set profile she knew for sure she would not get her way. Anger had collected in her throat and she swallowed in an effort to dislodge it. Should she threaten to leave? Supposing Bren let her leave? Where would she go? Don had said she could go to any of his family, but although she knew his offer was sincere she also knew there was no room at the cottage. His parents had an extra bedroom, granted, but if she went there how long could she remain? Suddenly her lip quivered and she felt helpless and lost. And a weight had already descended upon her at the idea of leaving Bren. Once she did leave him she felt certain she would never set eyes on him again.

'I d-did want my Sundays off,' she quivered, brushing a hand across her eyes. Slowly he turned towards her, frowning at her action. He was tensed, and still seething beneath the surface.

And then, miraculously, his expression underwent a change. A rare smile brought softness to his lawless features and his eyes lost their hard metallic light.

'Be a little patient, my dear,' was his cryptic advice. 'In a very short time you'll be having—more time to yourself.'

A pucker of uncertainty and bewilderment touched her brow.

'I don't understand,' she quivered. 'Please explain what you mean?' Why had he hesitated?

'Later.' The subject was closed by the finality of his

tone, but he clearly intended easing the strain for he said, regarding her now with a lazy expression as he leant back in his chair, 'What's all this aversion to marriage I keep hearing from you? I've said you're much too young and beautiful to be able to say you'll never marry. What reason have you for saying it? *Is* it aversion?' he went on curiously, 'or is there some other reason for your emphatic statements?'

She was still unhappy over his decision, for somehow she had been confident he would be obliging over the question of her Sundays. But his mood was too inviting to be ignored and she felt a compulsion to take advantage of it.

'I just know I'll never marry,' she answered obligingly, and a faint curve of his lips portrayed his amusement.

'Nonsense. How old are you?' A rather deprecating glance at her immature figure and then, 'Are you still eighteen or have you had a birthday since coming here?'

'I'm still eighteen. My birthday's not until August.'

'August, is it? What date?'

'The fifteenth.'

Bren fell silent and she had the impression that he was memorizing her birthday. The thought brought a happy smile to her face and she forgot her disappointment of a few moments ago. Noting the smile, Bren responded, and something caught at Laura's heartstrings. Would she always be content to worship from afar? Hitherto there had been love but no yearning, because she accepted the remoteness between them, knowing Bren was totally unaware of her very existence ... but now he was aware of her existence, and now the remoteness no longer separated them...

They had tea together, just the two of them, in the sitting-room by the fire, and for the first time since coming to the Abbey Laura forgot her melancholy surroundings, and the evil that had invaded this dark house so very long ago and remained in occupation. The firelight glow was mellow and soft; it played on her companion's features and erased the harsh lines from round his mouth and softened the granite-like set of his jaw.

'Was Aunt Margaret's headache very bad?' she inquired when it became clear that she would not join them.

'I didn't ask her how bad it was,' he returned indifferently, and Laura then asked if she ought to go up and see how she felt.

'She might be glad of a cup of tea,' she remarked, looking at him questioningly.

'If she wants tea in bed she'll ring for it.' There was a note of finality in his tone and Laura allowed the matter to drop. Apparently Bren considered it unnecessary for her to go to his aunt, so she gave herself up to the pleasure of having Bren all to herself for a while.

Lady Margaret came down later in the evening and a glance of hatred passed between her and Bren before he rose and left the room.

'Did you enjoy your walk, dear?' The change was staggering. Laura nodded and said yes, she had thoroughly enjoyed being out.

'Is your head completely better now?' she then asked.

'Not completely, but much better than it was.' A slight pause and then, 'Were you terribly disappointed, dear, at not going out with Francis this afternoon?'

Laura became guarded. She was not being drawn into the hatred existing between Bren and his aunt. In any case, she was not disappointed, so she had no intention of satisfying Margaret by saying she was.

'It didn't matter either way. I enjoyed my outing, as

I said.'

'But it was lonely for you, surely?'

The woman's transparency afforded Laura a slight measure of amusement. Clearly she wanted to convey to Bren the information that Laura had suffered by his action.

'I wasn't alone, Aunt Margaret,' she replied. 'I went to the cottage to see my friends.'

The eyes became veiled, but Laura sensed the woman's anger at receiving this most unsatisfactory answer to her question.

'I should have thought you'd become homesick, keep going along to the cottage the way you do?'

'Sometimes I feel unhappy about losing it, yes. But Matt and Lucy are good to me and I can do as I like there. They've told me to carry on treating it as my home.'

'But this is your home,' sharply. 'I told you that when you came. This is your home for always, Laura, remember that, won't you, dear?'

The 'dear' seemed out of place, for the woman's eyes were narrowed and her tone was curt and hard.

Laura made no answer, for Francis entered the room at that moment. His mother turned and asked where he had been.

'Just driving,' he returned carelessly, and poured himself a drink.

'It's a long while to have been driving around all on your own?'

'I stopped at a café for tea.' The glass was drained and he poured himself another drink. He still didn't seem to be very well, thought Laura, noting the strange dullness of his eyes. She had seen it often before, though, and after he had rested it had disappeared. He would be in bed until after lunch tomorrow, she knew, and then he would probably be all right again.

'Sit down,' his mother said, as if she too had noticed he was still looking off colour. 'Bren's high-handedness spoiled your day, didn't it?' Her eyes moved from him to Laura, as though including her despite Laura's assertion that she had enjoyed herself.

'He was right; I was ill and I shouldn't have been driving.' He took possession of the chair by the fire. 'I've damaged the car, so he'll have something to say about that, I suppose.'

'Damaged the car?' Lady Margaret stared interrogatingly at him. 'You mean, you've had an accident?'

'Oh, neither of—— I wasn't hurt at all. Just hit a damned tree that was too near the road.'

That was a close thing, thought Laura—and she didn't mean the accident. However, his mother had apparently not noticed the slip, for she inquired as to the amount of damage done to the car.

'Wing ripped off—or almost off,' he replied without much concern. 'Bren's got plenty of money to put it right.'

'There'll be a fuss, though. You shouldn't have been so imprudent—knowing you were going out today . . .' Margaret tailed off, her eyes straying to Laura, who was staring at her, her wide brow creased in a frown of puzzlement. 'What I meant,' she went on to explain to Laura, an unaccustomed flush rising in her dark face, 'is that Francis wasn't well the night before and—and he should have stayed in bed until lunch time today.' She looked away, and her voice weakened at the end of her sentence.

Laura's eyes moved wonderingly to Francis. She had seen him drink but had never seen him the worse for drink. But she was remembering two things now as she watched his fingers twitching as they curled themselves round the glass he held in his hand. She was remembering that forbidding glance sent by Bren to his cousin when Francis was about to pour himself a drink of whisky, and she was remembering Mr. Dodd's joking remark that one or other of these two might be a secret drinker...

CHAPTER EIGHT

THERE was to be a ball at the castle. Lady Margaret and the two men received invitations; three days later Laura received an invitation too. She wondered by whose hand such a clever manipulation had been made, and decided it was Bren who had obtained the invitation for her. The idea that he would go to this trouble afforded her some considerable pleasure and when after lunch one day she found herself alone with him she smiled dazzlingly at him and murmured her thanks.

'I never, never expected to find myself the guest of an earl!' she added, although her proud head was held in such a way it would almost seem she considered she had every right to be among the noble personages who would be attending the ball. 'Every time I look at the castle from outside I long to go in,' she went on confidingly when Bren did not speak. 'I always imagine it to be associated with wild heroic deeds, don't you?'

He smiled then, and the almost perpetual mask of cold indifference was lifted. She looked hard at him, remembering that profound and fleeting interlude when, in the garden, she had uttered his name involuntarily and he had smiled in just the same way he was smiling now. She remembered the silence which followed, a strange unfathomable silence during which they were caught in a web of unity and drawn close. Yes, she herself had been drawn irresistibly to Bren ... and she knew for sure that he also had been affected in a similar way. Could it be within the realms of possibility that the strength of her love for him would gradually penetrate and affect him? The idea that he might one day come to love her was something on which she had never dwelt, for he seemed as remote as the stars. And yet a Dewar had once before found all he desired in a girl like her. It would be nothing new for history to repeat itself. It was natural that she should flush at such thoughts as these and Bren watched her half-questioningly, the smile still playing about his thin-lipped mouth.

'Wild heroic deeds?' he repeated, amused. 'You once told me you were a romantic, I seem to recall. As a matter of fact Hulnworth Castle was—in the barbaric days to which you're referring—fortified by one of the many barons endeavouring to maintain some semblance of authority along the line of the Border.' Wild laws were then in existence, he went on to tell her, and these were disregarded by even wilder men, men who had so come to accept the life of desperate enterprises and savage devastation as their proper lot that they knew only contempt for the Lord Wardens who would have had them control their inherent craving for blood.

Her eyes glowed as he continued with his narrative. The Border was to her a thing of intense fascination. She never experienced the slightest difficulty in conjuring up a picture of life in those times when even the religious communities had to rely for their security on the strength of their fortifications. For no one either side of the Border was safe—neither the sturdy barbaric Scots nor the bold men of Northumberland. There were always occasions when one side would shrink in mortal dread of the other, and the surviving lofty walls of Northumberland encircling some ancestral home or priory were sufficiently significant of the lawless character of Border life in those early days of robbery and murder.

But today the lovely castle stood in the peaceful setting of a Northumbrian town, whose ancient square was tree-shaded and whose people, having long since forgotten all about such emotions as jealousy and envy, moved slowly and contentedly about their business, for there was no need for haste in this mellowed spot through which meandered the lovely tree-lined river and from whose surrounding hills could be seen some of the most magnificent scenery in the whole of the country—the great volcanic mass of the Cheviots forming in part a natural barrier between England and Scotland, the beautiful Vale of Whittingham and the grassy banks of the River Aln, the heights of Teviotdale; and, on a clear day, the sad and memorable high ground of Flodden could easily be discerned. And in another direction, towards the sea, could be distinguished the castles of Bamburgh and Dunstanburgh, and closer to, the little floating rock of Coquet Island.

'If I could choose another age in which to live,' murmured Laura after a little silence, 'it would be in those stirring times of such gallant exploits.' She was seated on the couch, while Bren reclined in a great damask armchair some distance away from her. The sun slanted through the window picking out the fiery strands of bronze and copper from among the glorious dark-brown of her hair. Bren watched her inscrutably, noting the delicacy of her face, revealed to him in profile, and the long curving sweep of her dark lashes as they threw shadows on to her cheeks.

She turned to him, awaiting some comment on her remark and he said unemotionally, yet with a hint of humour in his eyes,

'Those gallant exploits, as you call them, were invariably followed by summary retribution. Your entire family could have been wiped out in a single night.' As he ended his humour became more pronounced and Laura blushed, experiencing no difficulty in imagining what he had left unsaid. The 'whole family' embraced the males, of course. Females in those days were carried off by whichever side was victorious. He noted her blush and a faintly sardonic twist came to his lips; her blush deepened, but she made no attempt to avoid his gaze as she wondered once again what it would be like to be carried off by him. No mercy could be expected; no sensation of pity would halt or even soften his actions ... She shook her head unconsciously. Had he lived in that bygone age and, victorious, had snatched her from her family, he would have known only contempt for her helplessness and would have crushed her completely, unswayed by feminine tears or despairing implorations. And yet today she felt so safe with him, still sure that no harm could ever befall her while Bren was there. 'My child,' he said suddenly with a little smothered laugh, 'what are your thoughts that they bring such an expression to your face?'

His question and his relaxed manner startled her somewhat even though of late he had begun to take much more interest in her. But she did not concern herself with wondering at this new and unexpected attitude because he was staring at her and obviously awaiting an answer to his question. Her eyes twinkled and she caught her lower lip between her teeth as if to suppress the laugh threatening to escape—for she knew it would be a distinctly self-conscious laugh which could just provide him with a clue as to what had been running through her mind.

'I—I was only thinking about the Borderers and the way they acted——'

'Such as?' The interruption was accompanied by a mocking lift of one eyebrow. Laura had a shrewd suspicion that her guard was superfluous—that already he had probed her mind.

'Well, such as assaulting their neighbours and—and indulging all the while in that predatory warfare...' Her voice trailed off into silence because he was inwardly laughing at her and deriving amusement from her obvious discomfiture. But her sense of humour responded after a while and she laughed then, even though it *was* a self-conscious laugh, as she had known it would be.

'And abducting their daughters,' he submitted, flicking an imaginary speck of dust from his sleeve. Her eyes flew to his.

'So you *had* guessed what I was thinking.' Not all of it, she hoped! Not the part where she personally was involved.

'You're very transparent. Your blushes gave you away.'

She breathed again. He had not guessed all.

'I suppose you've met the Earl many times,' she remarked conversationally, deciding it was time to change the subject.

'Several times, yes.'

'I can't imagine your liking a function such as we're going to.'

'I abhor such functions.'

'Yet you're going?' A quiver crept into her voice. Supposing he should change his mind and decide not to go. Her whole anticipation had centred on his presence at the ball; already she had danced in his arms, feeling their hardness against her. She had savoured the joy of his clasp upon her hand, had looked up to see his dark face above her—had even drawn a smile of admiration from him!

'Yes, I'm going.' He became harsh all at once and dejection dropped upon her momentarily. Interludes like this were precious owing to their rarity. She had no wish for this one to end yet awhile. His dark eyes flickered strangely at the change in her expression. He asked her the reason for it and this time she made no effort at prevarication as she said,

'I thought you might change your mind and not go.'

A short silence followed, and then Bren said, an odd

note in his voice,

'Is it so important that I go?'

She nodded, and for a moment a smile trembled on her lips. His harshness had disappeared as swiftly as it came; she was not curious as to the reason for it. It had gone, and that was sufficient to restore her spirits.

'It wouldn't be the same without you,' she told him, her brown eyes wide and frank. 'I should feel very strange if you weren't there.'

Another silence, this time it lasted much longer ... and while it did last the harshness reappeared upon Bren's dark face. Laura frowned. What was he thinking to make him look like that?

'Francis would be there,' said Bren at last. 'How could you feel strange?'

'It wouldn't be the same. Oh, I'm quite comfortable with Francis, but—but I want you as well.'

Wordlessness again, stretching out the seconds into minutes. Bren seemed a long way off, thoughtful and tense, his mouth compressed, his eyes like embers suddenly fanned and ready to burst into flame. His emotions were aroused in a rather frightening way; he was as restless as on the day he had taken her up into the wild regions of the Cheviots. She sensed a terrible combat taking place within him, tearing him apart. What was wrong? she wondered fearfully. Her face went pale and as this registered with him he returned to her, leaving the struggle and becoming almost relaxed.

'You're pale, child,' he remarked, but at this her colour began to return slowly to her cheeks. She smiled at him in a rather sweet and childish way; he responded, and they both suddenly recalled that moment in the garden. Bren was, strangely, the one to lower his eyes, and while she sat there, wondering why he should avoid her gaze like this, he spoke to her abruptly, telling her to go and put on her ball dress.

'Put it on, now?' She looked blankly at him, only to see him nod his head and hear him say in tones fringed with impatience,

'Yes, now. I want to see it on you.'

She took exception to this order and her chin tilted loftily. But even as she opened her mouth his eyes glinted darkly, and dangerously.

Laura rose from her chair and went to do his bidding.

A few minutes later, in her bedroom, she twisted before the mirror, holding out the wide stiff skirt of padded silk. She arched her neck proudly, and smiled. There was no mistaking that she was of the aristocracy. Bad blood there might be in the Dewars, but there was blue blood too.

She went downstairs silently, her dainty shoes of silver kid making no sound on the carpet. She entered the sitting-room and stood in the doorway a moment, fully aware of the picture she made. Was she flirting with Bren? she presently asked herself as she gave him a radiant smile, showing a row of perfect, milky-white teeth. Her long hair fell dazzlingly on to her shoulders, and there was a luminence about her lovely eyes he had never seen before. She became profoundly aware of his scrutiny, of the examination of her whole body from her head to her feet, and when his gaze finally rested on her face she again flashed him a smile, then glided forward, floating like some beautiful ballerina towards the centre of the room.

Bren continued to stare at her face, yet no move nor mannerism escaped him. Something twitched at the side of his jaw, like a nerve out of control. Laura stood still some distance from him, baffled by his silence and the depth of his interest. Suddenly his eyes smiled, without obliterating any of the harshness portrayed in his face.

'Come closer,' he invited softly, and rose to his feet.

Laura obeyed and he extended his hand. Overcome with shyness, she stepped back and said lightly, swinging her slender body around,

'Do you think it's a good fit?' She had her back to him, but she was brought round by his firm warm hands on her shoulders.

'It's a perfect fit.' A pause and then, 'I'm buying this for you, Laura.'

She shook her head; he had offered her the money the day she brought it home from the dressmaker's, but she had refused to accept it. Lady Margaret was paying her wages now and Laura had bought the dress with this money, plus some of her own which she still had left from the sale of her few belongings.

'It isn't right,' she began, when he interrupted her.

'Laura...' Dangerously soft the voice; his eyes glinted and she saw him now as she had seen him on his first visit to her cottage, haughty, imperious—a man who plainly considered himself a superior being. 'I said I'll pay for the dress.'

For no apparent reason she felt the prick of tears behind her eyes. If he were intending to pay for it then why treat her like this—detracting from her pleasure at the gift by his arrogant domination and coldness? She had been holding the dress up from the floor, but she let it slip from her fingers and instinctively brushed a hand across her eyes.

'All right,' she said unhappily as he waited, towering above her, for the capitulation he meant to enforce. 'You—c-can buy it.'

'Why all this misery?' he wanted to know, diverted. His hands were still on her shoulders, his eyes still fixed on her face. 'You're a funny child, Laura. What have I done—tell me?'

She looked down at her skirt; it just touched the floor.

'If you wanted to pay for it then—then you should

have offered in a nicer way—well, that's what I think,' she added as she felt him stiffen.

'I see.' Bren's fingers automatically moved over her smooth white shoulders. 'I'm sorry,' sardonically, and then, 'May I buy the dress for you, my dear?'

She blinked at him and shook her head in bewilderment.

'I don't understand you,' she whispered, picking up her dress again and wondering abstractedly if she ought to have an inch taken off the bottom.

'There isn't any reason why you should understand me,' returned Bren indifferently. But then he began talking about hair-styles, saying she should have her hair up.

'Like this?' She brushed it up with her hands, holding it scraped away from her face. Some fell down and Bren swept it back. Their hands touched; both let go of her hair as their bodies came close. The next moment Bren's dark head was bent and she felt his cool clean breath close to her mouth——

Swiftly he moved as the door opened and Margaret walked into the room closely followed by Francis. Bren, all cool confidence, sat down on the chair he had previously vacated. Laura on the other hand turned a flushed face away from the new arrivals. Had Bren been about to kiss her? She recalled his other kiss and its utter lack of meaning. Would this one have been different?

'What's going on here?' Francis was in a strangely high-spirited mood and she wondered if he had been drinking. 'My, but you look a smasher in that!'

Margaret waited in silence for Laura to turn around, which she did, darting a glance at Bren, who smiled and said,

'You may go and change now. I've satisfied myself that the dress is all right.'

Margaret regarded Laura's flushed face for a long

moment before saying, to Bren,

'Why should you desire a dress rehearsal? I told you the dress was all right. Laura showed it to me when she brought it home.'

'I wanted to see it on,' he snapped. 'For so important an occasion as this we must make sure everything is just right.'

His aunt's lips compressed, but before she had time to produce some biting retort her son was speaking. He appeared to be a trifle dazed now, and quite oblivious of any tension that might be in the air.

'What colour would you call it? Yellow——?' He made for the nearest chair and occupied it. 'Or is it gold?'

'Gold,' snapped his mother. 'Trimmed with pearls.'

'Imitation pearls,' corrected Laura unnecessarily. She was thankful to be recovering so quickly, for her nerves had become all tensed up while she waited breathlessly for the kiss that never came.

'Go and take it off,' ordered Bren quietly. 'And to-morrow go into Alnwick and have the hairdresser put up your hair. I want to see what it looks like.'

Laura shot him a speaking glance as she turned. Much as she loved him she was not going to be ordered about like this. Why couldn't he have *suggested* that she go to the hairdressers? Did he still consider her a child, as he had done on their first meeting? True, it wasn't so very long ago, but he did know her a little better now.

Feldon flitted past the door as she emerged from the sitting-room and she jumped, her heart thudding.

'You're a creepy, weird sort of man,' she whispered silently as she hastily made for the stairs. Feldon had given her the shivers ever since that very first day when in her fright she could almost have believed him to be a ghost. And sometimes he would look so strangely at her, peering from colourless eyes as if intently looking for something. 'I wouldn't like to find myself alone with him,' she said to her reflection a moment later as she took off her gown. 'He could commit murder, I feel sure.'

Little did she know the important part Feldon was eventually to play in her life.

Reflecting on what Bren had just said about her hair, Laura stood before the mirror and began pinning it up. Very distinguished, she decided with satisfaction. Tomorrow was Thursday ... would she be allowed to go into Alnwick in the morning? she wondered. She had promised Lucy she would mind the baby in the afternoon so that she could do her shopping unhampered by the pram.

'I'm not letting her down, even for my hair-do,' said Laura to herself, her lips pursing determinedly. She would have ventured the question of when she was supposed to go for this hair-do, but for the arrival of Margaret and her son. Laura felt she would have more chance of success if she waited until Bren was alone before asking for the morning off.

Lucy stared in astonishment and admiration.

'You look like a duchess!' she exclaimed on seeing Laura's hair-do. 'What's the idea?' Kevin had been restless during the night and she had him in her arms. 'Now if it were next Tuesday I could have understood it.'

A laugh fell from Laura's lips.

'That's what it's for—the ball. But Bren wanted to see what it would look like first. He wants the French pleat altered slightly,' she added, turning her back to Lucy. 'He said it should be about an inch to the left.' She turned again and marked the odd expression on her friend's face.

'He's taking an extraordinary interest, isn't he? And how particular—an inch, indeed!'

'He says everything must be just right.' Laura's eyes sparkled. 'I want it to be so as well. Oh, Lucy, it's going to be the most wonderful night! Everybody's going!'

'Everybody who is anybody, you mean,' laughed Lucy, sitting down and rocking Kevin on her knee. 'I expect all the aristocracy of Scotland will be there too.'

'Yes, I expect they will.' Laura went out to hang her coat on a hook at the bottom of the stairs. 'The dust! I'm sure you're fed up with it all,' she remarked on returning to the living-room.

'It'll be worth it. The stairs have to be altered, naturally, and that's what's causing the dust and sand to be all over the place. They've had to knock through the wall in order to give access to the new bedroom, but the workmen say it will all be done in less than a week.'

'Less than a week! They haven't taken long. Is it a month since they began?'

'Just over.' Rising, Lucy put Kevin in his pram and pulled up the covers over him. 'Let's hope he continues to sleep,' she whispered, turning to Laura. 'You don't mind looking after him?'

'I love minding him. And don't worry, Lucy. If he does cry I'll nurse him.'

But Kevin didn't cry and Laura was able to enjoy herself in the kitchen, where she baked cakes and pies, and then put the kettle on in readiness for Lucy's return. They might just have time for a cup of tea before going along to the village school to pick up the two girls.

With a little while still to spare Laura went into the sitting-room and stood looking at the wall over the fireplace, memory flooding over her in spite of the fact that the whole atmosphere of the room was changed by bright paint and wallpaper and by the deep red carpet on the floor and the new curtains and furnishings. Suddenly aware she was no longer alone Laura turned.

'Don—oh, how you scared me!'

'Sorry, Laura...' His eyes were on her hair and it was clear that his opinion did not coincide with those of Lucy and Bren. 'What on earth have you done to yourself?'

Blushing at his outspokenness, she lifted her chin. 'It's for the ball——'

'For the ball?' he interrupted, staring at her. 'The ball isn't till Tuesday.'

'Bren wanted to see what it looked like first. If he hadn't liked it I'd have had to try another style.'

'Would you?' His mouth went tight, but all he said was, 'I can't say it suits you, Laura. It's too old a style for you.'

'But the occasion's so formal,' she explained. 'I have to look—well, sophisticated, if you know what I mean?' He didn't and she swiftly changed the subject, asking why he was here at this time of the day.

'I finished a job and decided not to make a start on another until tomorrow morning.' Automatically they moved into the other room. 'Where's Lucy?'

'Out shopping. I've been minding Kevin.'

'And baking, unless my sense of smell is teasing me.'

She laughed, breathing a sigh of relief at his change of mood.

'I'll make some tea. Do you want cakes or pie?'

'Both.' He followed her to the kitchen, watching as she plugged the kettle in. The electricity had been connected only a couple of weeks and Laura could not make up her mind whether she liked it or not. There was something attractive about oil lamps with their soft illumination, but she did realize they weren't practical where there were children. 'I suppose you're very thrilled about this ball at the castle?' Don's voice was strangely sharp again and she turned, a shadow crossing her face. She had firmly asserted to Bren that Don was not a special friend... but she now knew he would like to be more than a friend. Yet he seemed to be held back from any demonstration and for this Laura was glad. Don was a very good companion and she would feel a deep hurt should anything come between them.

'Yes, I am thrilled, naturally.'

He stared broodingly at her. 'They're all going—the three of them?'

She nodded, and reached up for the crockery that stood on a high shelf.

'I'll put three cups and saucers out; Lucy will be on the bus——' She glanced at the clock. 'It'll be here in a couple of minutes.'

Don picked up a plate and put some of the cakes on it.

'What sort of pies have we?'

'Apple, and gooseberry. The gooseberries are out of my—out of Matt's garden.'

'You've just picked them?' Don took the gooseberry pie into the other room.

'No, Lucy had them ready.' Laura followed him with the tray. 'We'll wait for her,' she said. 'I think I heard the bus a moment ago.'

'What do women find to buy!' exclaimed Don when Lucy entered, her arms full of bags and parcels, and a huge shopping bag hanging from one arm.

'What are you doing here?' she wanted to know, dumping her load on the couch.

'I finished that job at the shop and it was too late to start another. What on earth have you been buying?'

'Oh, all sorts of things. It's Lynn's birthday a week on Sunday, you know, and I've got her a present. I've also been buying candles and decorations and heaven knows what for the party.'

'You didn't say she was having a party.' Laura poured Lucy a cup of tea and the elder girl took it from her as she sat down on a chair by the fire.

'I thought I did. Anyway, you're invited.'

Don cast Laura an odd glance and then,

'Will you be able to get out?'

'I think so. Francis will be asking me to go with him, I suppose.' Since that Sunday when Bren would not allow Laura to go out with him Francis had never again been 'ill'. Whether or not his indisposition on that occasion was the result of alcohol she had never discovered, nor had she seen Francis the worse for drink—although often he would remain in bed until lunch time, or even later. His mother would say he was off colour, but always there would come to Bren's face that expression of sneering contempt. However, so long as she could get out on Sundays Laura was not concerned with anything else Francis might or might not do.

When, much later, it was time for Laura to go home, Don offered to walk with her to the gates of the Abbey. Dusk had fallen, and an admixture of purples and greys enveloped the landscape and cast shadows over the sea. The rocky crags on which stood the Abbey became dark and sinister, the Abbey itself was merely another black shadow in this world of oncoming darkness.

Don slipped an arm around her shoulders as they walked through the village; not another person was to be seen, and suddenly he stopped and turned to her.

'Laura ... I'd like to kiss you——' He shook his head. 'Dare I?'

The darkness hid her blushes. She thought of Bren's kiss, and her own awakening. That kiss had meant nothing to him, though. He kissed her just because she happened to be there.

'You did once before,' Laura shyly reminded Don at last.

'I did,' he sighed, and there followed a long, rather disturbing pause before he spoke again. 'At that time there were things I didn't know.'

'What things?' Don was holding her hands in his and she sensed a slight nervousness in the sudden movement of his fingers. She recalled her earlier impression that he had a secret and would like to talk to her about it, but that he refrained for some reason. 'Tell me about these things.'

The night was closing in on the last moments of dusk, the sky was showered with a million points of dazzling crystal and a crescent moon hung in their midst. It could have been a romantic situation, but both Don and Laura were tensed.

'I can't,' said Don at last, and Laura frowned at the break in his voice. 'I'd like to, but—no, I can't.' And he did not kiss her after all, but began to walk on again, swiftly, as if he now wished to leave her as quickly as he could.

CHAPTER NINE

BREN drove the car along an approach enclosed by battlemented walls and high grey turrets. Sitting beside him, her heart beating quite abnormally so great was her excitement, Laura stared in admiration at the great castle, standing on a hill, with the river winding about beneath its massive walls. Soon they were passing through the entrance gateway, surmounted by a portcullis above which were two gigantic towers. The grand quadrangle was next approached, entered through a lofty arched gateway flanked by towers, and once through this the castle loomed before them, its appearance grand and imposing with lights glittering from every window and floodlights directed from its turreted walls on to the gardens where fountains were illuminated and coloured lamps hung from the trees.

They were greeted by the Earl and Countess, and many were the eyes turned in Laura's direction, for she made a regal figure, her head held proudly on aristocratic shoulders, her throat and hair adorned with Laura Vernon's magnificent jewels.

A short while later, dancing with Bren in the great baronial hall, Laura could not help musing on the past and what the first Laura Vernon had missed. But for a whim of fate she would have known many scenes such as this, would indeed have become one of the aristocracy.

Laura's musings were brought to an abrupt end when on passing the table where Lady Margaret sat talking to an acquaintance, she surprised a look of such open hostility that she actually gave a start, falling out of step.

'What is it——?' Bren broke off, following the direction of her gaze. Laura dragged her eyes away, an icy shiver running along her spine, marring the pleasure of the dance. Bren swung her round and she looked up at him. The dark features were twisted into sadistic lines, but the expression in his eyes was one of triumph. Laura frowned, struck by a sudden thought. Lady Margaret had said coming along in the car that she hoped Laura and Francis would dance together most of the time. They made such a striking couple and her own enjoyment would be increased just by watching them and feeling proud of her son.

But up till now Bren had made sure that Francis had not claimed Laura for any of the three dances, and even now, as the music stopped, he said, obviously not requiring an answer to his previous question, 'Do you think it's becoming a little warm in here? I'm finding it a trifle stuffy. Shall we go outside for a breath of fresh air?'

So she wasn't to be partnering Francis for the next dance, it seemed.

They went out into the gardens, into the warm night air where a soft breeze caught the perfume from thousands of roses and wafted it gently towards them. Stars shone brightly from a clear purple sky and the silver radiance from a lambent moon bathed the distant hills and valleys in light, while the grounds themselves were brilliantly illuminated by the floodlights and the lamps strung in the trees.

'Lots of people are out,' remarked Laura, her heart acting strangely because she was so profoundly aware of the man beside her. Immaculate he was tonight, with a gleaming white dress shirt contrasting vividly with the deep tan of his skin, and a perfectly-tailored suit which accentuated his leanness yet gave the impression of concealing powerful muscular strength. He took her hand in his and Laura reached the pinnacle of happiness as they strolled like this through the lovely grounds of the ancient castle. In the days of the third earl these grounds had been remodelled by that magician of landscape styling, Capability Brown, when the formal groves and parterres were replaced by groups of forest trees and wide rolling lawns. Random shrubberies took the place of immaculately-clipped yews; and the prim walks, flanked all along by lead statuettes gave way to herbaceous borders and colourful rock gardens.

'There's a seat over there——' Bren indicated a rustic bench under a drooping Japanese cedar tree. 'It's about the only one that's vacant.' They increased their pace and sat down just as another strolling couple espied the unoccupied seat. 'You're right,' agreed Bren, looking round. 'Lots of people are out.'

Contentment such as she had never known settled upon Laura and instinctively she moved closer to her companion, not fully conscious of her action until it was too late. Turning his head, Bren looked curiously at her . . . and was it imagination or was there a slight regretful shaking of his head? She could not know, and yet a strange uneasiness assailed her, bringing a tiny frown to settle between her eyes. If Bren noticed it he chose to ignore it as he asked if she were enjoying her first ball. His voice lacked its familiar coolness and that little access of disquiet vanished as she replied, her tones soft but eagerly enthusiastic,

'It's wonderful!' She turned impulsively, a flush on her delicate cheeks, her eyes as clear and shining as the brightest star in the sky. 'Thank you for bringing me, Bren.' An ardency entered her voice and he threw her a frowning glance. Then all hardness left his face as his eyes widened with a sort of dawning perception. Her pulse quickened. What had he guessed? she wondered uneasily. The ensuing silence became charged with tension as, still frowning, Bren continued to regard her, his eyes searching with such intensity that she felt he were endeavouring to read her very thoughts. The silence took on an oppressive quality, with Laura bewildered by his attitude and seeking for words while Bren himself appeared to be holding words back.

At last, with a deep sigh that was totally out of character, Bren rose from the seat and, reaching for her hand, brought her up beside him.

For a brief moment they stood there together, and it seemed to Laura that Bren fought an inner battle with himself, that he was being mentally tortured by a state of indecision. It was a moment fraught with drama and uncertainty. A difficult smile broke at last, but Bren ignored it and they continued to stand there, under a starlit sky, Laura small and deceptively fragile, her hair like a glorious crown, her mouth quivering and her soft brown eyes as limpid and trusting as those of a fawn. In sharp contrast the tall angular figure of Bren seemed overpowering. His dark features were lawless, his eyes had reverted to their customary hardness. The wind had freshened and the branches of the cedar tree swayed, sending long thin shadows down his face so that it appeared to be streaked with evil black scars.

'Come,' he said at last, his tones curt and hard. 'It's becoming chilly; we'll go back inside.'

He retained her hand as they re-entered the castle through an open window of the Blue Drawing-Room. One other couple was in possession, seated at the far end of the vast apartment. Engaged in intimate conversation, they did not even notice the entrance of Laura and Bren, and after a perfunctory glance at them Laura gave herself up to an examination of the room, glad of the diversion and the chance to open an impersonal conversation. For she was still a little uneasy as to whether Bren had made a guess at her feelings. He appeared to have done so ... and he did not appear to be exactly happy about it. Perhaps she was mistaken, she told herself a little desperately; perhaps she was just imagining things. She sincerely hoped she was.

Looking around her, Laura gave a little gasp of admiration. The evidence of wealth took her breath away. The wallpaper was Chinese, and two hundred years old, Bren informed her. The furniture was French, some of it coming from the Château des Tuileries; the ceiling was ornately decorated with flowers and trees and animals. Magnificent ornaments and groups in Sèvres china stood on the wide marble mantelpiece and on various occasional tables; the walls abounded with priceless paintings by Reynolds and Van Dyck.

'You wouldn't think it was a castle, would you?' A sweeping gesture of Laura's hand indicated the lovely walls and ceiling. 'Not this part, at least.'

Bren seemed amused as he said, watching her curiously,

'You like all this luxury?' He walked over to a couch and sat down, still holding on to her hand. She drew her hand away as she took a seat beside him, careful this time not to sit too close.

'I think it's marvellous.'

'Very far removed from your humble little cottage.' An odd inflection in his tone and she looked at him. His face was impassive, but a throbbing of a nerve in his cheek betrayed some inner tension as he waited for a comment from her. She made none and he added, 'You were happy in your cottage? You prefer something small?'

She frowned. It were almost as if he were asking her if she *wanted* a cottage.

'I would always choose my own cottage in preference to anything else,' she told him frankly. 'I loved it, as you know, because of the sentimental value it had for me.'

He spoke sharply. 'Don't you think you can carry

sentimentality too far?'

She shook her head. 'We had lived with the atmosphere of Laura all around us. As I once said, we considered the cottage as a shrine.'

'But why?' still in the same sharp tones. 'Laura Vernon was just an ordinary woman——'

'Oh no. She attracted a man of the nobility——'

'Nell Gwynne attracted a king,' he reminded her dryly. 'What makes you insist that Laura Vernon was unique?'

'I wasn't saying she was unique. But she must have had some extraordinary charm about her; also I believe she was unusually virtuous as well.'

'Unusually?' Bren raised his brows. 'In those days all women were expected to be virtuous.' He paused a moment, but Laura had lapsed into thought. 'In any case,' he added, still in the same dry tones, 'I wouldn't call an unmarried mother exactly virtuous.'

She lifted her face and frowned darkly at him.

'What a horrid expression! No one ever talks about an "unmarried father"!'

He laughed at her anger.

'But then a man is allowed more freedom than a woman.' His amusement grew as Laura's brown eyes flashed. He reverted to the subject from which they had strayed. 'If ever you had to live by yourself again—you'd not be happy anywhere else but in your own cottage?'

'My own cottage...' she murmured, diverted. Her eyes were a trifle misty as they looked into his. 'You wouldn't have used those words once.'

Bren stirred uneasily. His glance strayed to the couple in the far corner, still oblivious of everything but their two selves.

'You know what I meant,' he said abruptly. And then, with strange insistence, 'Could you be happy anywhere else?'

Laura fell silent, considering this. The day must come when she would leave the Abbey, and she knew that there was a house somewhere—a house without any sentimental associations for her—where she would live. But Bren had asked if she could be happy. She spread her hands helplessly as his glance portrayed slight impatience.

'I wouldn't know. I expect if I had a home of my own it would gradually acquire a warmth and I should grow to love it——' Again she made a gesture with her hands. 'I don't know,' she repeated, her eyes rather too bright and her lovely lips quivering.

An uneasiness assailed him and he stirred in his chair as before. Unexpectedly he said, compassion dawning in the hard eyes perhaps for the first time in his life,

'You must try to forget Laura Vernon and the cottage, my dear. Nostalgia of this kind brings so much unhappiness in its wake.'

Was he sorry he had made her leave the cottage? she wondered. There was a brooding quality about him and she said impulsively,

'I'm getting over it now, Bren. And I'm not unhappy in your home.' She could not tell him the reason for saying she was not unhappy, but all unknown to her the radiance of love looked out from her eyes and the frown appeared on Bren's forehead again. However, before he had time to speak Laura was saying in dismay, having caught sight of herself in the mirror,

'My hair, Bren! It's falling down. Oh, what shall I do!'

'Falling down?' He looked at it. 'No such thing——'

'At this side.' She twisted round. 'What shall I do?' she repeated tragically.

'I'll see if I can fix it for you——'

'No! I'll go to the powder room and see to it myself. Oh dear, I hope no one sees me like this!' And the next moment she was gone, a screening hand pressed to one side of her head.

To her relief the damage was repaired without much difficulty and she returned to the Blue Drawing-Room within ten minutes of leaving it. But she halted in the doorway, for Bren was no longer alone. Sitting on the couch, very close to him, was a fair-haired woman dressed in a skin-tight evening gown of silver lamé, her face made up with immaculate care, her hair plaited round her head. At her throat and wrists diamonds shone, and there was a flash of crimson as she lifted a perfectly manicured hand to make an accompanying gesture to whatever she was saying.

After a long while Laura approached. There was an intimacy in the way they sat close and talked. Neither appeared to notice her and she gave a little cough. When Bren glanced up she had the extraordinary impression that he had in fact known all the time that she was there. Unaccountably Laura felt a loss of spirit.

'Ah, Laura...' Rising, he made the introductions and then indicated a place on the couch. She sat down; Bren was between her and Rita MacShane, but the woman leant forward, deliberately to examine Laura's face.

'She's staying up at the Abbey with you, you say? As a—er—guest?'

Laura looked sharply at her. Rita knew why she was at the Abbey ... she knew everything there was to know, of that Laura felt absolutely certain.

'Sort of,' replied Bren carelessly, and Rita's blue eyes flickered again to Laura.

Small talk ensued, with Laura suddenly realizing she was being left out. Her heart seemed to freeze within her; the evening was spoiled.

'Shall we go back into the ballroom?' Bren rose at last and Laura breathed a sigh of relief. Several times Bren had cast odd glances at her during his conversation with Rita, and Laura had the odd impression that he was curious to know her reaction to this more than friendly attitude he was displaying towards his old flame. And most certainly he was very different. He smiled at Rita and even took hold of her hand on one occasion. He leant towards her, he looked into her eyes with what could only be described as a lover-like expression. Laura might not have been there for all the attention he gave her. A fierce spasm of jealousy swept through her, and yet rising above this emotion was a strange sort of wonderment at Bren's unusual behaviour. Normally he was undemonstrative, and his smiles were rare. For him to act like this in front of a third person staggered Laura, for it was totally uncharacteristic. Inherently Bren was cold and unemotional; his feelings were never revealed, his face was invariably an inscrutable mask. Yet a miraculous change had taken place in a matter of minutes. It did not appear to make sense.

On reaching the brilliantly lighted banqueting hall Bren turned to Rita and, taking her in his arms, he whirled her away, leaving Laura standing there, alone. Her eyes followed the striking pair until they were lost in the moving throng, and then she made her way slowly towards the table where Lady Margaret was sitting. She was on her own, for Francis was on the dance floor. Margaret cast Laura a swift glance of perception before she turned her head to seek out Bren and his new partner.

'Sit down, dear.' She patted the chair next to her and obediently Laura occupied it. Bren's callous behaviour towards her shook her to the depths even while she told herself that she had always known he was callous. She searched for him on the floor, caught in a web of misery she had never remotely anticipated when, on driving to the castle by Bren's side, her heart had throbbed with sheer excitement at the prospect before her. He and his partner came close and as he saw Laura's misty gaze fixed upon him he seemed to hesitate a moment before, with a sort of deliberate gesture, he put his cheek against Rita's hair. Laura swallowed in an effort to remove the ball of misery settling in her throat. Margaret was speaking and she endeavoured to pay attention, but the tears pressed against the backs of her eyes, hurtful tears of disappointment and despair. Bren would marry Rita, there was not a trace of doubt in Laura's mind about that. 'I see Bren's found Rita—I only saw her myself a few moments ago. Don't they look happy?' Margaret paused, casting Laura another perceptive glance from under heavy lids. 'You seem upset about something, dear?' Laura merely looked at her companion and then averted her head. She was numbed with misery. 'Francis will be here in a moment or two and you can have the next dance together—— Oh, just look at those two—quite the lovers again after all these years. They used to be engaged, you know—but of course you don't. Well, they were, and some stupid little tiff resulted in their parting,' she informed Laura, quite unaware that Laura knew she was lying. 'It was a tragedy, because Rita in her pride went off and married a man who'd been running after her since long before she met Bren. The result was that they've both been unhappy ever since—that's why Bren never married, of course. He's always been in love with her. However, she's a widow now, so perhaps we shall be seeing some developments—it certainly looks like it, the way they're going on. Just look at them!' But her gaze was not directed at the couple about whom she spoke. It was fixed on Laura and nothing was lost on Margaret as she continued to watch the drawn young face in profile. She noted the tremor of the childish lips, the shadows darkening the soft brown eyes, the little throbbing movement in the temple.

As the evening wore on Laura became more and

more puzzled by Bren's behaviour, for although he appeared to prefer dancing with Rita—holding her much too close and often laughing down into her eyes—he also danced a good deal with Laura, and she was again convinced that his object was to prevent her dancing with Francis. However, Laura did dance with Francis several times and on each occasion she would notice the smile of satisfaction playing about Lady Margaret's lips. For Laura there was a tenseness in the atmosphere, especially when they were all sitting together at the table, having refreshments. On the surface Bren was charming to Rita and coolly indifferent towards Laura. And yet she sensed within him that restlessness he had shown on the day he took her up into the hills. He seemed to be passing through some state of mental upheaval where he was adhering with extreme difficulty to a decision already firmly made.

Immediately they had eaten their refreshments Bren and Rita slipped away and, watching them cross the wide floor of the ballroom, Laura saw them go out into the garden. She closed her eyes, unable to bear it as, just before stepping through the window, Bren slipped an arm around his companion's waist.

'May I have the pleasure?' Francis was speaking, a laugh in his eyes. Dumbly Laura rose and he whirled her away. They were the first couple on the floor and Laura blushed with shame as Francis repeatedly missed his step. He had had too much to drink, she felt sure, for his eyes were feverish and bulging, and his voice was becoming slurred.

One or two others danced with Laura, young men who wanted to know more about her, who flattered her and who sometimes held her far too close for her liking. They were dandies, some of them, men who had never known what it was to soil their hands. They were often feminine and mincing; they drawled with lazy boredom, were conceited and affected and adopted the most absurd mannerisms. Laura frowned as one persisted in trying to date her, clearly unwilling to take no for an answer. She had firmly declared she would never court a boy from the estate, but were these young men any better? Laura decided they were not.

'I say, why the teasing refusals? You known darned well you're going to say yes in the end.' The young man was fair and foppish; his hands were clammy and cold.

'I don't know what gives you the impression I'm teasing,' she returned frigidly. 'I'm certainly not going to say yes in the end. I don't want to go out with you and I'm telling you once and for all that I'm not going to.'

'My, but you're different from the rest! Do you know who I am?'

'I neither know nor care. And now, do you mind taking me off the floor?' She lifted her proud head and looked at him. 'I'm sure I can find more pleasant company than yours.'

Astounded, the young man led her off the floor and she sat down at the table with Margaret. They were joined by Bren and Rita within a few minutes and Rita said, with what Laura was almost sure was a touch of envy,

'You seemed to be making a hit with the Earl's son and heir. I'll wager there are plenty of young women here who could willingly scratch your eyes out.'

'The Earl's——?' Laura looked at Bren, who nodded. 'I didn't like him at all and I requested him to take me off the floor——'

'You ... what!' Lady Margaret looked at Laura aghast. 'No, surely you didn't!'

'I told him I could find more pleasant company.' Laura glanced at Rita. The girl was regarding her through narrowed eyes, taking in every noble line of her face and the high forehead above fine aristocratic brows.

'How dreadful!' exclaimed Margaret, clearly distressed. 'You shouldn't have done that, Laura. Everyone will be talking about you.'

'If he has any pride he won't mention it,' commented Laura carelessly. 'I know I wouldn't, if someone snubbed me like that.'

'Why did you snub him?' Bren spoke quietly, his eyes never leaving Laura's face.

'He kept on trying to date me and wouldn't take no for an answer. I've no time for such people!' The haughty voice was a feminine counterpart of Bren's at its most pronounced and Rita said, turning to Bren,

'I haven't yet quite placed Laura. You say she's a guest...?' No mistaking the subtle inquiry as to Laura's lineage, and Bren said quietly,

'Laura is a relative of ours. We're second cousins——' He threw Laura an amused glance, and added, 'Or is it third cousins?'

She merely shrugged and looked away. He had hurt her unbearably this evening and she could not trust herself to speak to him, for she felt certain she would burst into tears. The emptiness within her had grown out of all proportion and she felt as if she would never be happy again as long as she lived.

The drive home seemed unbearably long. Bren cast a sideways glance at Laura now and then as if he would read her thoughts. She was aware of these glances but did not return them. In one short evening her life seemed to have been shattered, for she could see the picture as a whole, the swift courtship and marriage, could see Rita installed at the Abbey...

'I can't bear it,' she whispered convulsively. 'I can't bear to think of Bren married to anyone else!' And to Rita... That was even worse than the thought of his marrying someone Laura could like. Rita MacShane she could never like, not in a hundred years. She was cold and hard—and how could she ever have loved Bren when she could go off and marry someone else, someone with a title? Surely Bren had more sense than to be taken in a second time—— Laura checked her train of thought as it was borne in on her that Rita was possessed of immense attractions, for in addition to her facial beauty she had a most seductive figure and, of course, the sophistication and assurance of age. For the first time in her life Laura felt inadequate, lacking confidence in herself.

Immediately on arrival at the Abbey Laura said a brief good night which embraced her three companions, and went upstairs, conscious of Bren's eyes following her right up till the moment she was lost to his sight on turning into the corridor leading to her bedroom. Within a few minutes the lovely gown was lying on the floor where she had stepped out of it; Laura Vernon's jewels lay on the massive oak dressing-table and Laura was in bed, in the darkness, her face turned into the pillow, sobbing as if her heart would break.

CHAPTER TEN

THE sea was warm and still. Laura lay on the sands, her slender limbs exposed to the sun, while Don swam about a little way from the shore. There had been an unusually hot spell and the beaches of Northumberland, normally rather cold for sunbathing, had been attracting small crowds for the past three week-ends.

Laura waved in response to the brown hand which came out of the water. It was just two months since she had sought the help of Don's brother and sister-in-law and she was now occupying the new bedroom which had been built on to the cottage. But this could not continue, she had known that right from the start. The bedroom had been intended for the two girls, while Kevin would have occupied the tiny room in which Dodie and Lynn were now sleeping. Kevin was in a cot in his parents' room, but of late he had been easily disturbed, with the result that he was wakened on his parents' entering the room, and sometimes it would be the early hours of the morning before they got him to sleep again. So gradually Laura had come to accept the fact that Laura Vernon's jewels must be sold. It was a heartbreaking decision and many were the tears Laura had shed over it. But now she was resigned and tomorrow she would go into Alnwick and see about selling the jewels and at the same time consult an estate agent and ask him for his lists of property. She had noticed there was an estate agent in the block of offices to which Bren went on the day he had taken her into Alnwick with him.

Tears filled her eyes at the memory of that day. So happy she had been, all oblivious of the plans he had made for her future.

Absently Laura scooped up a handful of golden sand and let it trickle through her fingers. Would she ever be able to forget that moment of revelation?—that moment when her heart seemed to be held in the icy fingers of death, so shattering was the knowledge which Feldon had imparted to her on that unforgettable night, the night Bren had fallen from his pedestal, bringing her whole world crashing down with him. He would never know how she wept that night, alone in the darkness of her dismal room.

She turned and smiled as Don came out of the water. He sat down on the towel she had spread for him and reached for another with which to dry himself.

'Why so pensive?' he wanted to know, his boyish face set in a frown. 'It's the problem of your future again, I suppose?'

She nodded, fully aware that, given only a small degree of encouragement, Don would see that her future held no problems at all. But he knew of her feelings for Bren, because they could not be hidden when she was pouring forth her story and asking for the help that had been so solemnly promised by Don and of which Laura had been so confident she would never need to take advantage.

'I'm going to sell the jewellery, Don.' For a long while she had kept the fact of its existence a secret from her benefactors, but a few days ago she had told them about it, because in any case her ready cash was running low and she would have been forced to part with something in order to carry on, for she insisted on making a payment for her keep, even though both Matt and Lucy firmly asserted she more than earned it by her work in the house and garden, and in looking after Kevin while Lucy resumed the part-time job she had had when they were all living with her husband's parents and she had been able to leave Kevin in the care of his grandmother.

'You're going to buy a cottage?' He looked away, the towel idle in his hands. 'Where, Laura?'

Where . . .? Far, far away from Bren she wanted to go . . . but there were her friends.

'I thought perhaps I could get one somewhere near Alnwick, and then work in the town.'

'Work? What at?'

She bit her lip. 'I've no idea, Don. But obviously it must be easier to get work in the town. There's nothing in the village.'

'Why must you leave Matt and Lucy? They want you to stay, you know that.'

'I'd love to make my home with them,' she admitted frankly. 'But it isn't possible. They need that room. It was built on especially to ease the situation and while I remain at the cottage they're no better off than they were before.'

Don rubbed his arms with the towel, his eyes on the sea, dark and brooding.

'If only—if only——' He stopped, sighing deeply.

'I've always loved him, Don,' she said gently. 'I'll never love anyone else.' It was difficult to say these words, but she must impress upon him once and for all that there could never be anything more than friendship between them. She gave him a smile—a wise little smile, for she knew that what he felt for her was deep and sincere pity and anxiety—nothing more, although she was fully aware that he himself was convinced that what he felt for her was love.

'How did you come to fall in love with a man like that?' he demanded, suddenly angry and almost overbearing in his manner.

She shrugged.

'You know it all, Don. You heard that I used to watch him when he was out walking—that was what you meant when you told me you understood. Do you remember?'

He nodded.

'Yes. I'd heard about it from Matt.' He looked at her. 'Didn't it worry you that people knew you went out of your way just to—well, to look at him?' He seemed embarrassed and Laura smiled. She it was who should have been embarrassed, but strangely she was not. Hadn't Mr. Dodd said, 'People *know*, young Laura'? And hadn't Crossley said only a few moments previously that it was known that she saw Bren every morning? Far too late now for embarrassment. Her love for Bren had been common knowledge in the village for some time.

'I've never been particularly concerned about other people's opinions of me,' she said truthfully. The Dewars never were, she could have added, but refrained.

'I suppose I was really sure you cared for him when you were so indignant when I asked if you trusted Bren implicitly.'

She did blush then, and lowered her head.

'I—I believed I could trust him—with my life, as I said.' Two great tears welled up. She should have known right from the first why she had been taken to the Abbey, for it was only too apparent, but in her blind adoration she had put such faith in Bren that the idea of his harbouring such a dastardly idea as that of marrying her to a drunkard and an imbecile had never for one moment entered her head. And yet everyone else knew. Mr. Dodd knew, she thought, recalling how he had warned her to take care and hinted that someone was going to be very disappointed when all the cards were thrown on the table. *She* was the one who was disappointed—— Her mouth curved bitterly. Disappointment was a mild word for her feelings when Bren's perfidy was made known to her, for she had felt her heart was breaking.

It was three weeks after the ball; Margaret had gone to see her aunt, remaining out until very late at night.

Rita called at the Abbey, where she received from Bren all the attention she could have desired. She stayed for dinner, a meal which proved most uncomfortable for Laura, for Francis was also absent, having been in bed the whole of the day. She knew why he was 'off colour'. Earlier she had heard Bren slating Feldon for leaving the wine cellar unlocked...

Watching Bren and Rita at the dinner table Laura felt convinced they were in love. Yet still Bren's manner puzzled her. Never would she have believed he could act in this way; he was attentive, he was charming and smilingly indulgent. Rita for her part used her eyes—which Laura grudgingly owned were extraordinarily beautiful. She touched Bren's hand when speaking, she laughed a lot ... and both she and Bren behaved as if Laura were not there at all.

The moment the meal was over Laura made her escape, going up to her room.

'What about your coffee?' Bren had said as she excused herself and rose from the table. Laura merely looked wordlessly at him, her great eyes reflecting the pain in her heart. He had swallowed thickly, she remembered later when she was in her bedroom, sitting on the bed, staring into space. And his hand on the table had closed so tightly that the knuckles shone white through the transparency of the skin.

For a very long while she had sat there, an unbearable ache in her heart. She had a vague impression of a car starting and driving away. Bren taking Rita home. She rose and looked down at the lovely jewellery she had worn at the ball ... the ball that was going to be so wonderful, she had excitedly told Lucy. The remainder of Laura Vernon's jewellery was in the drawer, Bren having given it to her on her request, so that she could choose which pieces she would wear at the ball. Opening the drawer, she drew the rest out and laid it beside those already lying there. How much would they fetch . . .? With a gesture of complete abandon Laura put her face in her hands and wept. Why had Rita come back into Bren's life? Why couldn't things have remained as they were for a long long while to come?

A sudden noise behind her brought her hands down; through the mirror she saw Francis, his eyes burning and seeming to protrude right out of their sockets. His mouth was twitching spasmodically, and a white froth was gradually building up around it. Laura's own eyes dilated. She turned, stepping back as Francis made a silent entry into the room. She tried to scream, but terror blocked her throat. However, she did manage to articulate words after making a tremendous efforts to clear her throat.

'Francis, it's Laura . . . you wouldn't—you wouldn't harm me, would you?' He drew nearer; Laura was against the dressing-table and could go no further. There was no one in, she thought, beginning to speak again, urgently, her voice cracked and high-pitched. 'We're friends, aren't we? You and I are friends——' The rest died in her throat. Fear dropped from her, but her legs were still like jelly. 'Feldon . . . thank God!' Never would she have believed she would be so thankful to see this ghost-like old man who had so often by his mere presence sent tinglings running down her spine.

'It's all right, miss, he's quite harmless.' Feldon turned to Francis and took hold of his hand. 'Come, it's in your bed you should be——'

'The lady—I only want to talk to the lady.'

Laura shut her eyes tightly, her heart contracting with pity for him.

'The lady wants to go to bed, and that's where you're going. Come, I'll help you to undress and you'll be asleep in no time at all when you've had the drink I'll make for you.' The voice was so gentle, so kind and

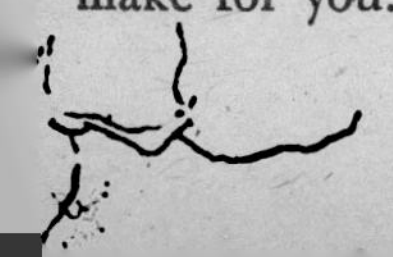

understanding, that Laura bit her lip, almost drawing blood, so ashamed did she feel. She had avoided Feldon whenever she could, had almost run from his presence whenever she found herself in it. 'Say good night to the lady.'

'Can't I talk to her?' Francis took another step towards Laura, but Feldon's grip on his hand drew him back again.

'Not now. Tomorrow, perhaps.'

Francis smiled. Feldon took out a handkerchief and wiped the froth from about his mouth.

'All right, tomorrow, then. Good night.'

'Good night,' she stammered, tears rolling down her cheeks.

Twenty minutes later Feldon knocked on her bedroom door. She opened it on hearing his voice saying,

'Don't be afraid, miss, it's only me.'

'Yes?' She still felt white and shaky, but her chief emotion was pity.

'May I come in and speak to you for a moment?'

'Of course.' How could she ever have been afraid of him? she wondered. He was so old, and so frail in appearance. 'Would you like to sit down?' She indicated a chair and he took possession of it.

'Thank you, miss.' A small pause and then, 'The room you saw—it's never been used since Mr. Francis was a youth. He's absolutely harmless now—just like a child when he has these turns, which occur very rarely indeed. But of course you weren't to know all this——' He looked at her and smiled. 'I hope he didn't scare you too much?'

A smile fluttered in response, but unconsciously Laura put a hand to her throat.

'I was very glad to see you,' was all she said, but her words held a wealth of meaning.

'I'm sorry. It was all my fault. You see, I knew the attack was coming and I meant to lock his bedroom

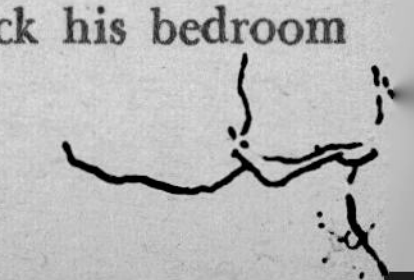

door. Mr. Bren will be furious when he knows you've been scared.'

Feeling she now knew why the old man was here, Laura quickly assured him that Bren would never hear of the oversight from her. Feldon was shaking his head.

'It doesn't matter, miss. You've no need to shield me, for I'm leaving at the end of the month—going to live with my widowed sister in the Cotswolds.' He fell silent a moment, concern on his pale lined face. 'It's because I'm leaving that I've decided to speak, miss,' he continued at last. 'I don't owe it to her ladyship to keep quiet, for she's never treated me like a human being. I might be a dog, the way I'm addressed by her. Nor do I feel obliged to remain silent for Mr. Bren's sake. I can't feel I owe him any loyalty, for he's a hard unfeeling man.' He frowned in thought and Laura mused on this odd position in which she found herself. After having shrunk from this old man—perhaps even displaying to him her nervousness and dislike—she was now feeling most kindly disposed towards him and smiling as she waited for him to come to the point, for it was clear that he had something of importance to tell her. 'Do you know why you were brought here, miss?'

She started, instantly recalling all her little tinges of apprehension on first coming to the Abbey. She recalled the subtle hints of Mr. Dodd and of Don; she remembered what she had overheard in the conversation between Lady Margaret and her nephew. Every incident flooded into her memory as she said in a rather quivering voice,

'To be Lady Margaret's maid-companion.'

The old man smiled faintly. 'Her ladyship never had a maid-companion before. No, you were brought here, miss, as a prospective bride for Mr. Francis. They planned it, I heard them talking about it long before Mr. Bren made you leave the cottage. Her ladyship was threatening to marry Mr. Francis to the gardener's red-faced wench and there was a big row over it. Then that business of yours over the cottage brought you to Mr. Bren's notice—— Are you all right, miss? You've gone very white ...'

The old man had talked some more, telling Laura that Bren and his aunt had hoped that by throwing Laura and Francis together Laura would fall in love with Francis. Feldon had wanted to tell Laura the truth for some time 'because she was a fatherless little lass all on her own', but two things deterred him. First, Laura herself had made it difficult for him, he had told her half apologetically, at which she flushed and apologized, and secondly he had to think of his job. Had he informed Laura of the plot against her and had it come to Bren's ears then he, Feldon, would have been instantly dismissed. But as he had now decided to retire Feldon had nothing to fear and so he was letting her have the truth for what it was worth.

'I've seen for some time that you weren't partial to Mr. Francis,' he went on. 'And who would be partial to a man like that? I'm sorry for him, but he brings it on himself to a certain extent. You see, he's a heavy drinker, and it's only when he's been on the drink that he gets these fits. Mr. Bren's never had any sympathy for his cousin because, being of excessive strength himself, he can't imagine why others should be weak. Francis is his own worst enemy, I'll admit, for he squandered all his inheritance—and his mother's, for that matter—on drink.' So much was explained as Feldon talked and Laura felt she must have been quite blinded by her love not to have realized what was going on. 'If you take my advice,' said the old man finally, 'you'll get ourself away from here. The Dewars always were a bad lot and they'll go on being that way till they become extinct, and that shouldn't be all that long, for Mr. Francis won't ever marry and if Mr. Bren married Mrs. MacShane there won't be offspring, because if she's not had children in ten years of marriage it's clear that she doesn't want them.'

Laura's reflections were cut short by Don's reaching out and taking hold of her hand.

'You've been thoroughly disillusioned by Bren Dewar,' he said gently. 'But you'd heard all the rumours about him and his family. You should have guessed there was an ulterior motive for their taking you up to the Abbey.'

She nodded, thinking of Bren and his complete lack of interest in what was happening to her. On the morning following Feldon's disclosure she waited until Bren had gone off with Crossley and then she had called a taxi. Feldon met the driver at the gate and told him to skirt the front of the house and stop at the servants' entrance, for Laura felt so physically ill that she had no wish for contact with Lady Margaret.

The note which Laura had left for Bren had never been acknowledged even though she had informed him where she would be staying.

'I should have known, yes,' she admitted miserably at last. But she had trusted Bren so, would—as she had told Don—have trusted him with her life.

'Must you leave Lucy and Matt?' Don's voice was softly persuasive, and edged with concern. 'You can't live alone, Laura.'

'I lived alone after Father died.'

'You were in your own village; you knew people. In Alnwick you'll feel so very strange.'

'I shan't be far away from Lucy and Matt, and although it's a good distance from your parents I can still visit them. There are plenty of buses.' There was a firm accent of decision in her voice and eventually Don shrugged.

'I'll help you, then. When are you intending to begin this house-hunting?'

'Tomorrow. I'll find out first how much my jewellery's worth, and then I can give the house agent some idea of what I can pay.'

Laura sat quietly by the fire, waiting for Don. Lucy and Matt had gone to a party and Don was to come and sit with Laura until they returned, when Matt would then run him home in the car. The children were in bed and all was silent, just as it had been when she and her father used to sit by the fire, reading, Laura thought, a catch of pain in her heart. Why did things have to change?

An hour later she began to wonder what had happened to Don, and by the time the clock struck nine she realized he was not coming.

What had gone wrong? Perhaps one of his parents was ill, or perhaps Don himself was not feeling too well. Laura settled down with a book, and at half past ten decided to go to bed. She left a note on the table saying Don had not put in an appearance. Then, after fixing the fireguard, she went up to her room above the garage.

Smoke wakened her, thick black smoke curling up the wall. Choking and coughing, she shot out of bed, calling frantically to Matt and Lucy.

'Wake up—there's something on fire downstairs——' She was on the tiny landing. God, the whole house was ablaze! 'Matt——' She passed the girls' room, flinging open the door as she did so. 'Lucy, for God's sake, wake up...' Laura's voice failed her. Matt and Lucy weren't in yet...

'Auntie Laura!' Dodie was screaming and clinging to her; Lynn was half-way downstairs, but could get no further as flames shot up from the tiny space by the front door. Vaguely Laura heard voices, chattering voices and calls of,

'Throw the children out—we'll catch them! *Throw the children out!*'

'Auntie Laura ... Auntie Laura ...' Lynn was sobbing, seeming unable to move as she watched the flames licking the stairs, coming closer with every second.

Hampered by Dodie, Laura did at last manage to throw open the landing window, and, picking up the terrified child, she dropped her into the spreading arms of Dick Peters, a burly farmhand from the Dewar estate. By the time Laura had Lynn at the window a blanket had been produced and the half-fainting child was caught in it. Kevin ... Laura put her nightdress to her mouth, for she felt her lungs must surely burst before she reached the room in which Kevin lay, crying loudly in his cot.

'Laura's in there on her own,' she heard Dick Peters say. 'I've just looked through the garage window and the car's out.'

'Poor lass—— Laura, are you all right?' It was Mr. Dodd's voice; Laura tried to shout, but she felt she was suffocating. Weakly she managed to reach the window, and Kevin was thrown through it. 'Now you, lass. Jump! Nothing to worry about—jump, girl, the whole place is ablaze!'

'What's she waiting for?'

'Jump, young Laura—— What's wrong with the girl?'

'She must have fainted. Oh, why doesn't the fire brigade come!'

'Shouldn't be long. Bill Travers rang for it as soon as we saw the flames. Walking home from the Crown, we were ...'

Laura was in the room over the garage, frantically gathering together Laura Vernon's treasures into a cover she had snatched from the bed. There would be some breakages ... the lovely groups ... the clock and the Madonna and Child ... the jewels——

'Laura! Laura, jump! Where are you!'

She stopped what she was doing, her whole body stiffening and suddenly feeling icy cold in the midst of all the heat around her. Bren's voice . . . It came again, but it was so dim. The smoke poured into the room now; she caught sight of her face in the mirror—begrimed and drawn. She returned to her task.

'Laura, are you there? Answer me!'

'I'm afraid she's been overcome, sir.'

'She'll be a goner if the fire brigade doesn't arrive soon.'

The treasures were all in the bedcover and Laura began struggling with the portrait of William Dewar, dragging it towards the window. Would there be time? There must be time! Laura Vernon's treasures were not going to perish! Thank heaven this room was over the garage; it would be the last to catch alight.

'Go in, sir! Are you a-wanting to commit suicide!'

Go in . . . Laura stopped, her heart leaping right up into her throat.

'It's a furnace. You can't go in there, sir!'

'He means it—hold him, Dick!'

'Take your hands off me!' So imperious the order, given in a voice harsh and cracked. 'I'm going in!'

'No!' Laura flung herself towards the window and opened it. 'No, Bren, you mustn't——'

'Darling—thank God!' The babble of voices ceased at these words and in the glare of the flames Laura saw that the villagers were staring at Bren in open-mouthed astonishment. He was oblivious of the sensation he had caused. 'Laura my love, jump—jump into the blanket, dear.'

Had ever such tenderness been expressed in a man's voice? Laura peered down into his face.

'The portrait, Bren—and Laura's——'

'Jump, dearest!' he interrupted urgently. 'Never mind about anything else. There's not a second to lose! Jump out of the window!'

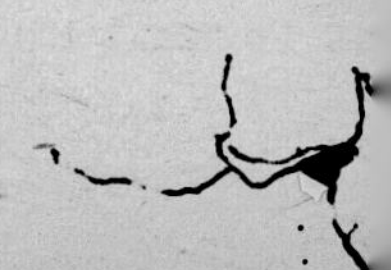

'Yes——' She turned on hearing a crash. The door had fallen inwards; she was aware of a million sparks of fire, of the frantic voice of Bren calling, calling from such a long way off . . .

She came to in the hospital in Alnwick. Bren was sitting by the bed, his face tired and drawn, but touched with a softness she would never have believed possible. Every detail of the nightmare happenings came back in a flash.

'You—you called me—called me—darling,' she whispered, just as if nothing more dramatic had ever taken place.

'My dear——' He seemed to have difficulty in speaking, so strong was the emotion that gripped him. 'Laura, whatever's happened in the past, whatever my intentions at first, I want you to know that I love you.'

'Love . . .' She could not doubt it, for she knew he must have entered the cottage and brought her out, risking his life for her, and she closed her eyes tightly. Bren loved her; it was too much to accept without some show of emotion, and from beneath her long dark lashes two great tears spilled down on to her cheeks. 'How long have I been here?' she asked, shy all at once and making for safer ground.

'Only since last night——' He glanced at his watch. 'It's not yet lunch-time. You came round soon after they brought you in, but they immediately gave you a sleeping draught. You've slept well.' He asked her how she felt and she wriggled about under the bedclothes.

'Fine. I wasn't hurt, apparently.' She looked at him. 'And you weren't, either. It was a miracle.'

'Indeed a miracle,' he echoed fervently, and took her hand in his. The tenderness of his expression and his touch filled her with a sort of exquisite pain because she desperately yearned for more. She desired his arms about her, his kiss upon her lips. Again she took refuge from her emotions by resorting to the prosaic.

'The children—they're all right?'

'Absolutely. I've not seen them, of course, because I've been here since last night. But Matt and Lucy called about an hour ago and I was talking to them. They're coming to see you later today.' He paused. 'They're deeply indebted to you,' he added, stroking the back of her hand with a tender, caressing movement.

Laura shook her head. 'They needn't be. The fire was my fault. I obviously didn't fix the fireguard properly.'

'The fire could have been caused by a faulty plug. Lucy was saying that the one in the kitchen used to get hot, and according to those who arrived on the scene first the fire started in the kitchen.'

'So it wasn't my fault?'

'I don't believe it was, darling, but it doesn't matter.' A great shudder passed through him before he added, his voice gruff with emotion, 'Nothing matters except that no one was hurt.'

She looked up into his dark face and her cup of happiness was full. She no longer avoided the important issues as she said,

'There's so much I don't understand, Bren.' Her lips parted invitingly as the last word was uttered and he bent his head and kissed her, tenderly, and yet with a possessiveness that both thrilled and excited her. And then he began to talk, admitting that his first intention was to encourage a marriage between her and his cousin. But very soon he had changed his mind and this led to increased friction between him and his aunt, who still hoped for the match.

'Do you remember that day in the garden?' he asked suddenly, and she nodded. 'That was the beginning of love, but I ignored it. I wasn't good enough for you, I told myself——'

'Not good enough!' she interrupted hotly, and smile of tenderness touched his lips.

'No, Laura, I didn't consider myself good enough for you. And I ignored my feelings—or perhaps I should say I suppressed them. But I knew I must get you away from the Abbey and the first thing was to find you a little home of your own. My mission in Alnwick that day was to see an estate agent——'

'Was that where you went?'

He nodded, and continued by telling her that he had in fact obtained a house for her and it was in the process of being redecorated when Laura left the Abbey. She spread her hands on hearing this, asking why he had not mentioned it to her.

'Because Aunt Margaret had already threatened to disclose everything to you and I wanted you away before she could do this. You see,' he added with a faintly bitter smile, 'although I felt at that time that I could never have your love, I did want to keep your respect. I knew you'd be horrified at what I'd intended doing, and it was my desire to get you away while you were still in ignorance of the real reason for our bringing you up to the Abbey.'

'Why did Aunt Margaret threaten to tell me everything?' Laura asked, puzzled.

'She had begun to suspect at my change of plan—and I also believe she knew I myself had begun to care for you. You remember asking for your Sundays off?' Laura nodded and he went on, 'I discussed it with her and it was then that she became suspicious. She said that the present arrangement must continue—that you must be encouraged to go out with Francis on Sunday afternoons.' He paused and she saw once again all the dark savagery of the Dewars revealed in his face. 'I was forced to let her have her own way because of her threats, but I was only biding my time, of course.' He paused again and Laura recalled her own astonishment that Bren could make such a weak statement as that his aunt needed Laura on Sundays. It was all explained now, as were so many other occurrences which had puzzled her at the time. 'If you remember, dear,' he went on at length, 'I did say that if you were a little patient you'd soon be having more time to yourself.'

'Yes, I remember. You had the house for me at that time?'

'The house, and a job. It was in an office in Alnwick, but there again I had to wait because it wasn't available just at that time. But my friend assured me he would take you on and I estimated that both the house and the job would be ready for you at about the same time.'

She shook her head. 'You were doing all this for me. Oh, Bren, I wish you'd told me!'

He sighed. 'So do I now. But as I've said, I wanted to keep your respect and I wasn't willing to run any risks with Aunt Margaret.' Raising her hand, he pressed it to his lips. 'And afterwards, darling, when I'd guessed that you loved me, I was even more afraid of your learning the truth, for I felt sure that in your disillusionment you'd run away—a long way away, and I would never know where you'd gone.'

'You guessed I cared, then?' And before he could reply, 'It was at the ball?' Bren nodded and Laura then said, a catch in her voice, 'Rita ... you left me f-for her. You appeared to—to love her ...?'

His face shadowed with remorse. But he explained that, believing himself unworthy, he wanted to kill Laura's love in infancy, whereupon she interrupted him with,

'In infancy! I've loved you for years!' And then she pulled up the bedclothes right over her cheeks, hiding their rising colour.

Bren stared at the pair of eyes still revealed.

'What did you say?'

She said something muffled under the bedclothes and he drew them away, repeating his question.

'You were William,' she told him in a faltering voice.

'William?'

'I used to wait for you in the woods every morning——' Laura tried to hide her cheeks again, but Bren held on tightly to the bedclothes. 'And—and I wrote about you in my little book.'

The most profound silence followed, and then, without caring a rap if the doctor or nurse should enter the little private ward where they were, Bren slid an arm under Laura's shoulders and, lifting her up, he gathered her to him, his lips finding hers and remaining there for a long long while.

'My little girl . . . what an utter fool I've been!'

'But you weren't to know,' she said reasonably, and invited his kiss again.

'Perhaps not, but I've still been a fool. You see, darling, that afternoon we had together after going into Alnwick was a time of struggle for me. I desperately wanted to tell you of my love and I see now that I should have done so—indeed I should! But all the while I knew I wasn't worthy of so sweet and innocent a child as you. I was remembering the bad blood of the Dewars and I at last decided that a boy like Don was what you wanted, and for that reason I never tried to contact you after you left the Abbey.'

She blinked at him. 'You always sounded as if you didn't like my seeing Don,' she reminded him.

'I was wildly jealous of him,' he admitted frankly. 'But, as I've just said, I decided he might be right for you.'

Laura nestled close, her cheek against his heart, and they were silent for a while.

'You kissed me that afternoon,' she murmured at

length, lifting her head to glance inquiringly at him.

'I really don't know why,' he had to admit after some thought. 'I expect it was something to do with my chaotic emotions.'

Laura told him she had sensed his strange mood and had concluded the kiss was merely a part of it. She refrained from mentioning that although it had meant nothing to Bren, it had in fact brought something physical into her otherwise pure and idealistic love for him.

After a while she returned to the question of the cottage, asking a question that had naturally been at the back of her mind ever since their conversation began.

'Laura Vernon's treasures . . . they're lost?'

'The place was completely gutted, Laura,' he told her gently, then added, 'Matt says several diamonds have been found and I daresay many more will be——' He paused, looking at her. 'Does it matter very much, my darling?'

She shook her head, realizing that both she and Bren could have lost their lives because of her persistence in trying to save Laura Vernon's treasures.

'No, it doesn't matter,' and she added softly, 'It's the end—the real end—of Laura.' Bren merely nodded and she changed the subject, asking where Matt and Lucy were at present. 'Back with Matt's mother?' she queried, wondering what they were thinking about Bren and herself.

'Yes, for the time being. I've another place, but it's been let go and it's practically derelict. However, I'll get a builder working on it and it should be ready in a couple of months or so.' He fell silent, absently caressing her smooth soft cheek with his. 'Laura dear . . .'

'Yes?' She leant away and looked into his eyes, her heart fluttering so that she felt he must be aware of it.

'I've decided to leave the Abbey—to make it over to Francis, along with a small part of the estate.' A slight pause and then, 'You'll be surprised to know that he has a girl-friend, and it looks very much as if he'll marry her.'

Laura flushed guiltily, and made a full confession.

'I didn't like deceiving you,' she added, 'but I did want to see my friends. And Francis had this girl—Meriel, so the arrangement worked very well.' She looked rather fearfully at him, thinking he must admonish her for her deceit, but he passed the matter off and reverted to the subject of the estate. Lady Margaret was all for a marriage between her son and Meriel, who had already been up to the Abbey several times. Although Bren refrained from making any reference either to Francis's drinking habits or his 'turns' as they were described by Feldon, he did say he hoped that Francis would take an interest in his portion of the estate and that hard work might be instrumental in changing his habits. He seemed extremely fond of Meriel, and Laura realized she had been mistaken when she had concluded it was only a passing affair—at least, as far as Francis's feelings were concerned. 'Where are you going to live?' she queried when he stopped speaking, and again her heart fluttered uncontrollably.

'Where am *I* going to live?' He looked at her, and said in a humble tone which she did not like at all, 'Laura dear, if—if you'll have me—if you believe I'm good enough——' She put a finger to his lips and said,

'I love you, Bren, and I want you.' So simple the words, yet so eloquent, and within seconds of uttering them she was gathered into his arms and his lips were pressed to hers.

'We'll have something smaller, and brighter,' he said at last, holding her from him and smiling tenderly at her. 'We'll have a happy house, darling——' He looked deeply into her eyes before adding softly, 'And we'll make our own memories.'

She knew what he meant—that she had carried sentimentality too far where Laura Vernon's cottage and treasures were concerned—and she nodded in agreement.

'Yes,' she whispered, her eyes radiant with love. 'We'll make our own memories.'